THE RUTHLESS GARDEN

Margaret Simons is the winner of the inaugural Angus & Robertson Bookworld Prize. Brought up in Adelaide, she took up gliding at sixteen and it was the landscape around Waikerie in the South Australian Riverland which inspired *The Ruthless Garden*. After completing university in Adelaide, she spent nine years on the Melbourne *Age*. She covered the Fitzgerald Inquiry and her stories on the Victorian Police internal investigations department were Highly Commended in the 1990 Walkely Awards. In 1991, she put aside her career to move to Waikerie and write *The Ruthless Garden*. Margaret is currently based in Melbourne and is working on her second novel.

THE RUTHLESS GARDEN

Margaret Simons

Published 1993 by Minerva Australia
a part of Reed Books Australia
22 Salmon Street, Port Melbourne, Victoria 3207
a division of Reed International Books Australia Pty Limited

First published in hardcover in Australia by
Angus & Robertson Bookworld 1993.

National Library of Australia
cataloguing-in-publication data:

Simons, Margaret, 1960–
The ruthless garden.

ISBN 1 86330 346 4

I. Title

A823.3

Edited by Sarah Brenan
Designed by Andrew Cunningham
Typeset in Berkeley by Bookset Pty Ltd, Melbourne
Printed by Australian Print Group
Maryborough Vic

CONTENTS

'To friends, starting with Jean,
Martin and Pat.'

UNDERGROUND

Deep flows the flood,
deep under the land.
Dark it is, and blood
and eucalypt color and scent it.
Deep flows the stream,
feeding the totem-roots,
deep through the time of dream
in Alcheringa.
Deep flows the river,
deep as our roots reach for it;
feeding us, angry and striving
against the blindness
ship-fed seas bring us
from colder waters.

— Ian Mudie 1940

Thanks to the Family of Ian Mudie for permission
to reproduce the poem 'Underground'.

CHAPTER ONE

JOURNEYS IN THE INTERIOR

I

Even before she accidentally-on-purpose got pregnant, Athena Masters was an enormous woman. Through adolescence she watched herself grow, and expressed conventional dismay at her size. She even dieted, but at the same time she pitied the little girls twitching in their tight skirts and high heels. She knew that size gave her presence. She was hard to ignore. She liked the flabby warmth of her own stomach and the folds of her copious flesh. She felt herself growing in body and power. The bigger she became, the more she felt she was in control. Chaos was outside, she thought, in the things she had not incorporated

At the age of twelve, Athena learned about the digestive system. The teacher drew blackboard diagrams of the body's orifices and the pipes that connected them. The mouth was done in red chalk and fringed with blue salivary glands, looking like little rain clouds.

Then there was the oesophagus and the pink balloon of stomach, the mess of small and large intestine and the end of it all, an anus: a coming together of the intestine at a break in the white chalk outline of the torso.

The teacher explained the need for all this, in animals the size of human beings. In really small organisms, such as amoeba, all the parts of the body were close to the outside. The cells could absorb and excrete directly. Larger animals were more complex and had specialised cells remote from the exterior. The digestive system, the lungs and the blood brought the outside world to the inside. They had the effect of increasing the body's surface area. Food and oxygen were absorbed and carried by the blood, which, pumped by the heart in a rhythmic surging, touched every cell. Anything not needed was expelled through the anus, or extracted then excreted by the rich, red kidneys and the bladder. Athena was fascinated. She drew arteries and veins in red and blue, and bile ducts in green. Afterwards, sitting lumpishly in the playground by the ant hill, she placed her fingers on her neck and felt the steady wriggling animal of her pulse. She was thrilled. She thought of her sandwich lunch swilling through her and being incorporated with her flesh

Years later, there was to come a moment when Athena felt that satisfaction again when, touching water, she felt she was connected with and in control of a deep wilderness. She was wrong.

II

The first white men to see the Ngawait country, later called the Riverland, were Captain Charles Sturt and his seven companions, four of whom were convicts. They came in the summer of 1830 in a whale boat loaded with guns, mirrors, beads and salt beef packed in barrels. They were searching for the inland sea. Instead they found the river, which Sturt named the Murray after some otherwise soon-forgotten colonial secretary twelve thousand miles away in London.

What Sturt did not realise was that the inland sea was there all along but, like so much about the ancient continent, it was hidden.

Charles Sturt, envoy of European civilisation, was brave and a good writer of journals, having been trained in the plain and manly prose thought suitable for young men destined to enter the military. He had soft cheeks and a big, slightly hooked nose. His hair was soft and wavy, his eyes wide open and pale blue, like a baby surprised by a loud noise. The light of the inland dazzled and eventually dulled those eyes. When his exploring days were over, Sturt became almost completely blind; a result, the doctors told him, of his journeys in the interior.

Sturt was a man capable of wonder, though not of irony. His mouth grounded his face. It was a straight, firm line: thin, with the palest pink lips.

Sturt and his companions began their journey on the Murrumbidgee in New South Wales. For weeks they sculled past banks closed in with reeds. Then one afternoon their boat shot suddenly out of the shallows of the little river and into a mighty green artery. This was the Murray. Sturt directed the men to hoist the Union Jack, and they stood up in the boat and gave three cheers.

In his journal that night, he wrote:

> *It was an English feeling, an ebullition, an overflow, which I am ready to admit our circumstances and situation will alone excuse. The eye of every native had been fixed upon that noble flag, at all times a beautiful object, and to them a novel one, as it waved over us in the heart of a desert. They had, until that moment, been particularly loquacious, but the sight of that flag and the sound of our voices hushed the tumult, and while they were still lost in astonishment, the boat's head was speedily turned, the sail was*

sheeted home, both wind and current were in our favour and we vanished from them with a rapidity that surprised even ourselves.

The current carried them on, past the mouth of the Darling, which Sturt had navigated in an earlier search for the inland sea and on into the golden cliff country of the Ngawait.

Here the current weakened and the river became more confusing, winding first one way, then the other, giving no clue to its eventual destination. Silence settled on the little boat as the cliffs rose on either side. They looked, Sturt thought, like the skulls of men piled on top of each other. The rippling of water against rock had eroded the softer parts of the stone and made hollows and cavities.

Because it was summer, the river was high, swollen with melted snow and monsoonal rains from the north. Food was plentiful and easy to get and the Ngawait were gathered in large groups. Sturt saw plenty of them. It was the time of the year when ceremonies were performed and social obligations met before the clan split into family groups and roamed the country more widely. As he had throughout his journey, Sturt handed out trinkets, unknowingly observing the laws which required payment for travelling through their country. Sturt was the first white man the Ngawait had seen, but the river people already had the white man's diseases, carried clan to clan from the fringes of the continent to the interior. Sturt wavered between fascination and disgust.

The most loathsome of diseases prevailed through-out the tribes, nor were the youngest infants exempt from them. Indeed, so young were some, whose condition was truly disgusting, that I cannot but suppose they must have been born in a state of disease; but I am uncertain whether it is fatal or not in its results, though, most probably it hurries many to a premature grave. Syphilis raged amongst them with fearful violence, many had lost their noses, and all the glandular parts were considerably affected. I distributed some Turner's cerate to the women. It could do no good, of course, but it convinced the natives we intended well towards them, and on that account, it was politic to give it, setting aside any humane feeling.

The Ngawait passed word down the river ahead of the party, so that each new group knew of their arrival. They were watched closely, but without animosity — strange, pale-faced visitors who posed no obvious threat. Some of the Ngawait followed Sturt's party for days at a time, often travelling more quickly on foot than he could by boat.

Sturt was impatient. He knew this artery must soon turn south to the sea, but each day their supplies ran lower, and the river twisted first south, then north again, then east and west, with the cliffs rising first on the left, then on the right.

One evening, he approached the party of Ngawait who had followed them for the last two days. There were three women and two elderly men. Sturt crouched down on one knee. It was a clear, warm night and the stars blazed above them, their brilliance only slightly diminished by the light of the campfires.

'Sea?' said Sturt, feeling slightly foolish. He was aware that he was talking louder than normal, as though this would penetrate the language barrier. 'Big water?' The two men looked at him, puzzled, and spoke briefly to each other. Sturt glanced around for some way to make his meaning clear. He pointed to the river. 'Water.' Then, looking for something to convey the idea of bigness, he pointed to the sky. 'Big. Big water.' There was no response.

He grabbed a stick and began to draw in the sand. The men and women gathered round: too close, Sturt thought, for comfort. He drew a wiggly line, meant to represent the river, then a boat containing eight stick-like figures. At the end of the line, he drew waves. The sea. Surely this should be obvious? Then, dropping the stick he held up his fingers. 'How many days? Five? Ten?'

He seemed to have got through to them. The older of the two men grabbed Sturt's stick and began making his own elaborate patterns in the sand — circles and lines connecting them, and more waves, like the sea. He got up and fetched more twigs and some leaves, and laid them carefully on the pattern. Then, like Sturt, he waved at the sweep of sky above them and spoke rapidly. Sturt stared at the ground. It made no sense to him. He was tempted, for a moment, to stamp on the arrangement, but of course that was foolish. The last thing he needed was to antagonise the natives.

Later, he wrote in his journal:

It was to no purpose that I questioned these stupid people. They understood perfectly, by my pointing to the sky and by other signs, that I was inquiring about large waters, but they could not, or would not, give any information on the subject.

The next day they sailed on downstream, the men in a stupor from the heat and the monotony of rowing. Sturt sat in the bow with his compass. It read south all morning, and his spirits rose, but then they came to a bend in the stream, and the cliffs rose on both sides. The only sounds were oars in water and the waves dashing against the base of the cliffs. Sturt groaned inwardly. His compass was reading west again and, as he watched, it swung further towards the north. He was careful to conceal his dismay from the men. In any other circumstances he would have feared mutiny, but here there was little risk. What choice did they have, but to continue downstream? The only alternative was to row upstream, which would be harder still.

The men sculled steadily, having adopted a pace they knew they could maintain. Their eyes were dull. The afternoon lengthened, and as the sun set the cliffs became brighter and brighter in colour, like dead gold.

For another three days they looped slowly between cliffs and floodplain, passing the sites of future towns. Then at last the river turned south, the cliffs subsided and the boat began the last straight stretch to the sea. Sturt passed out of the Ngawait country, and out of their story.

Six years later, on the strength of Sturt's testimony, the colony of South Australia was established.

III

One foot on the running board, the other burning in the pink sand of the paddock, Athena Masters was trying to get herself up into the driver's seat of the truck. Her cotton smock was hoisted around her hips, and sweat was running from every fold of her flesh.

They called it the red truck, although the sun had bleached and burned the paint into a mottle of matt pink on grey metal. Getting in had always been an effort for Athena. Now she was eight months pregnant, and she wasn't sure she could do it. She had used both hands just to place her thonged foot on the running board. She heaved again, her nose brushing the snakey blue veins on her thigh. Gravity was defeated! She was up, steadying herself with one hand on the steering wheel.

The truck was piled so high with bales of lucerne hay that the cabin and Athena were dwarfed. Before she had moved permanently to the farm, Athena had once taken a bale of lucerne back to Adelaide in the boot of her car, intending it for the garden. Her housemate Jean, accepting a lift the next day, had remarked that the car smelt as though something had died in it. Lucerne had a sweet smell, a little akin to that of rotting meat, but pleasant if you knew that it was not flesh, but hay. Now, the truck had been parked here at the highest, hottest point on the farm for hours, and the sweet smell was all around. Behind was the ribbon of highway and in front Athena could see the land dropping away to the pea-soup Murray River, the limestone cliffs rising, whitest gold, on the other side. The evening before she had gone down to the river to swim. The pelicans had taken off at her blundering approach, flapping and gliding into the cooling sky. Then the mosquitoes had come, and Athena was still itching from their bites.

From the running board, she could see Sam, a stick figure in blue overalls and orange towelling hat, working on one of the irrigation sprinklers in the paddock below. He spent a lot of his time unblocking or mending the worn and rusted parts of sprinklers. It was easy for him to see when a sprinkler had stopped working. Those that worked made green circles in the grey, as though someone had taken a compass, centred the pointed foot on the source of water, and drawn round. When a sprinkler was broken, the ground around it turned from green to grey in a matter of days. The charmed circle soon faded.

Sam had used all his savings to buy this farm, and had never had enough money to buy new equipment, let alone to wait for fruit trees and vines to establish themselves. Sam grew lucerne and grazed a few cattle.

Athena collapsed sideways on to the truck seat and then sprang up again. The vinyl was like a hotplate. She rummaged in the junk stowed behind the seat and found an oil-stained towel to sit on, then, grabbing and lifting her stomach with both hands, she pulled herself behind the wheel. Yes, she discovered, she could still turn it, which meant that she could make this trip. Sam could not afford the time to deliver the hay, or spare the money to pay someone else to do it, and Athena liked helping him. He wouldn't thank her, but he might come to need her a little more.

The day before in the Newera supermarket, Athena had met Rosie Thomas and said: 'I'll be bringing the truck up tomorrow to deliver that hay.' Rosie was shocked: 'Sam . . . he shouldn't let you. Like you are? He shouldn't make you,' and she nodded towards Athena's bulging stomach, pressed against the mesh of the supermarket trolley. Athena shrugged, her face haughty. 'He isn't making me do it. I do these things because I want to,' she said. Pushing her trolley, she proceeded down the supermarket aisle.

Now Athena turned the key, stamped on the accelerator and the engine started. Her stomach vibrated against the wheel and the gearstick pummelled her thigh. She fought the clutch to the floor and began to turn the truck towards the highway. Sam looked up at the sound of the engine and raised his hand to show that he knew she had managed, but of course he didn't actually wave and nor did she. Normally she would have worried about that, but she was happy today, with the sweetness of the hay about her, the journey ahead and the child stirring within.

The Thomas' farm was fifty kilometres up the river. In a car the return journey would have taken just over an hour but Athena expected to be away all afternoon. The truck was both proof and defiance of the proposition that everything tends towards chaos. Its tyres were nearly bald and its interior so cracked and filled with dirt and chaff that it seemed like a living thing. The truck hung together long after it should have fallen apart, and until it stopped going it would not be fixed. The engine overheated even on cool days, when there was no load. Behind the seat Athena had two jerry-cans full of water. She would travel slowly, and every twenty minutes or so she would have to stop, struggle down, let the motor cool and then fill the radiator. It was not a trip to be impatient about, she thought. As the tyres crunched off the gravel track and hit the hot blue bitumen, she thought that that was exactly the sort of journey she was in the mood for.

Sam's farm was on the edge of the Newera irrigation district, ten kilometres west of the town, set in country which was exactly the same colors as the map of Australia which he kept hanging on the kitchen wall: washed-out ochres, pinks and grey-greens, surrounded with bands of blue that intensified in color until they joined the great dark sweeps of ocean beyond the continental shelf. Those were the colors of the Riverland — hot earth, river, trees and most of all, sky. Judged by rainfall alone, this was semi-desert — part of the great plain that swept from the Adelaide Hills into the Simpson Desert. The highway that ran past Sam's farm began in Adelaide, led through the Barossa Valley, then down the grazed-smooth flank of the hills and on to the flatness. The further from the hills, the lower the annual rainfall. By the time the highway met the first of the Riverland towns, it was running through land where the wheat farmers got one good crop every five years, and the native trees by the side of the road were multi-trunked things barely taller than Sam's truck, their leaves turned away from the sun.

There was another color, of course, thanks to the river and to irrigation. Each Riverland town was surrounded by citrus green, the orchards rising sharply in ordered rows from the red sand, and the paler green of vines. One moment desert, then green. The highway ran west to east in a straight line from town to town but the river curved endlessly, sweeping away from the road, turning back on itself, taking fifty kilometres to cover ten. Most of the time, drivers on the highway could not see the river except when they were approaching a town. The towns clutched the swings and curves so that from the air they looked like deep green barnacles clinging to the humps and curves of a giant snake or sea-monster as it writhed its way across the plain.

The Riverland was a strange, tenuous place, not confident of its claim on the attention of passers-by. Each town announced itself to drivers with a roadside sign declaring itself as the 'Gateway to the Riverland'. First came Blanchetown, where you crossed the river; then there was a long dry stretch; then Waikerie (which was Aboriginal for 'wings'), then Newera, Kingston (named after a South Australian premier), Barmera, Berri (also an Aboriginal name) and

Renmark. Each was the gateway. Then you were out of the region and on the long dry haul to Mildura (which meant red rock) yet, according to the signs, you had never arrived.

Athena was on the highway and heading east. As she left the irrigation area, she passed one of the region's main tourist attractions — the Big Orange, three storeys high with leaves and a stalk on top. It had once been brighter than any real orange, but was now so affected by sun that it looked more like an under-ripe tomato. There was a viewing gallery on the top floor and a tourist shop at ground level. On one side was a fire-escape.

Athena had once commented to Sam: 'Why on earth have a fire-escape if you're trying to make it look like an orange?'

'Probably regulations.'

'What? All oranges more than two storeys high must have a fire escape?' and he laughed. That had been before she moved in with him.

Fifteen kilometres past the Big Orange was a little Lutheran church, built by the first settlers, painted white, and still in use. A noticeboard faced the road, erected in the hope of engaging some of the constantly passing congregation of traffic. This week the sign read:

ALCOHOL DOESN'T DROWN SORROWS. IT ONLY IRRIGATES THEM.

Athena shifted gears. The river had swung away from the road, leaving her driving in the dry.

IV

There are different ways of knowing a bit of land. For example, there are gardens. A keen gardener knows which vegetables grow best in which plot, and will see the caterpillar under the cabbage leaf, the mosquitoes gathering in the shady corner, the weed poking through paving, and the sappy growth from the rose bush that will have to be pruned in winter. The gardener knows each shrub, its needs and vulnerabilities, while the passer-by or visitor will register only the overall view, the shadiness and the greenery. Perhaps, if the rose bush is in bloom, the visitor might notice a flower.

A child will know the garden very well indeed, but in a different way. The child will see the crook in the tree where a doll might perch, or the knot of wood in the trunk where fairies might live. In the litter of leaves children will leave secret and powerful arrangements of twigs and gumnuts, which the adult gardener will trample over, or rake up for mulch.

Similarly, there are different ways of knowing a person. Gardeners know gardens in the way longtime lovers know their partners. Athena knew about the rough spot on Sam's left shoulder, and how his knuckles cracked. She could smell the differences in his perspiration, depending on what he had eaten the night before. Listening in the morning, she could follow his progress through the bathroom. She could gauge the strength of his stream of urine from the gush of it into the toilet bowl, and she waited for the tapping of the toothbrush on the side of the sink — once, twice — to shake off the water. After that the bathroom was free.

Yet for all that knowledge, such a lover can lose any sense of the impact the beloved makes when entering a room, or how they impress others. The delicate arrangements of personality, and the proud and secret requirements of the soul can be trampled upon, or never seen. Thus Athena misunderstood Sam, and Sam was mistaken about Athena.

For a few months when she was a child, Athena had an intimate knowledge of a small patch of dirt. Between the asphalt of the school yard and the grass of the oval was a bare slope, inhabited by a colony of ants. Athena had no playmates. She sat alone on this slope and, as the weeks passed by, began to watch the ants.

She stared at them for hours as they made their way in thin, particled lines down to the grass or up to the sandwich crumbs dropped in the schoolyard. She learned how an ant would negotiate its way around a pebble or a blade of grass or a damp spot, and she knew all the holes of the ant nest. Not only the obvious ones, surrounded by their cones of masticated sand, but also the more secret, secure holes, like the one in the little gully which was built on a slant into the hill, protected from the trampling of school shoes. Hour after hour, Athena watched the ants struggle up and down with crumbs. She dropped bits from her own sandwiches on purpose, just to see them lifted and manoeuvred under ground. She became so absorbed that she lost all sense of time. The noise of the schoolyard receded. She hardly ever looked up to see the sky, or her classmates' games. Often, she missed the school bell and came in late, rebuked by teachers and hissed at by the children. But at night in bed she thought of the bank and the ants and the grains of sand and the white pebble that lay in the middle of their track to the schoolyard. Tomorrow she would lift that pebble and put it aside, or throw it out of the ants' world altogether. They would be grateful, perhaps. What was it like, to tramp through those forests of grass, or to make one's way, like a busy body, under the scuffling, leather-clad feet?

Athena grew older, and her family moved house. She left the earth bank behind, and moved many times more, until as an adult she came to the Riverland and the farmhouse on the cliff, which (although she didn't know it) overlooked the spot where not so long before the Ngawait had come silently at dusk in their canoes of tree-skin, a little fire burning in the bow on a hearth of clay. They knew that pitted cliff. It turned golden in the afternoon sun. A man dived down at that exact spot. There, the Ngawait knew, was the underwater hole where the fish lived. The man placed a springy net, made from bark and rushes, over the hole and poked in with a spear. Out swam the fish into the net, as they knew it would.

V

Athena was sitting by the side of the road, her ears ringing from the noise of the truck engine. Now it was quiet except for the pinging and soft creaks it made as it cooled. In a minute she would open the bonnet, remove the radiator cap and, standing back so that the steam didn't hurt her, refill the radiator with water.

It was mid-week, so there were not many cars on the highway. The semi-trailers hurtled by from time to time, but for the most part the road was quiet and fiercely hot, running like a rough ribbon through the pink soil and grey scrub. In the heat haze, the dips between the sandhills looked as though they were filled with water but they were really very dry. Athena was staring at the sky. The mallee trees looked so sharp, as though the sky were a backdrop in a photographer's studio. Certainly now, at the height of the day, it glowed as though reflecting light, rather than being the source of it. But that was wrong as well, because the sky was not incidental. Compared to it, the land itself seemed insignificant, like dirt that had sunk to the bottom of a glass. The sky went on for ever, and the earth was only one of the things it was wrapped around.

A truck roared past, kicking up gravel. Athena shook herself. She had been dreaming. That was unusual, but today, for once, she wasn't anxious. It was easy to dream. She heaved herself up and refilled the radiator. It boiled over immediately but she kept pouring until it was still and replaced the cap. Then, using her hands to place her foot on the running board, she heaved herself back into the driver's seat. A car whipped by as she was mid-ascent, and the driver hooted at the sight of her suspended backside. Athena's face, at that moment pressed against the red vinyl of the seat, took on the same haughty look she had worn when talking to Rosie Thomas in the supermarket. It was a look those who knew Athena were familiar with.

There was an awfulness about Athena sometimes. She was difficult to live with. There was the ruthless way she did housework. She created a ferment in which only she could keep her feet. She lifted up the asparagus fern and shook it, sending dead leaves all over the floor. Then she would shake the string bag that held the onions, and the dry skins would go flying. When the floor was so full of debris that no one else could walk on it, she swept and mopped, remorseless in her reordering. Athena's old housemate, Jean, used to recline on the couch and feel guilty as the housework maelstrom descended, although they had a roster and it was not her turn. She would offer to help. Sometimes her offer would simply be refused. Other times, Athena would not even reply but would glower at her.

Once Athena's mother had come to stay and, after dinner, had washed up. She dipped Athena's china teapot into the suds.

'You're not washing my teapot up in the detergent are you?' Athena called.

'Well yes, of course I'm washing it up,' her mother replied.

Without another word Athena came, took the teapot from her mother's soapy grasp and rinsed it out five times with fresh water. Then, with angry little strokes of the knife, she cut up a lemon, put the pieces in the teapot and filled it with boiling water. Her mother stood helplessly, red hands clutching the dishcloth, as her daughter swung her big hips around the kitchen. The air was full of anger and strife. Jean felt oppressed. And the strange thing was that when they were alone Athena often washed the teapot in detergent. So what was it all about?

Athena had been a lonely child. Her father, a charismatic and erratic man, had what he liked to describe as a romantic soul. He had taken first to marriage and, when that ceased to excite, to drink. He had chosen Athena's name over her mother's objections. As part of one of the many courses he started and failed to finish, he had read Homer. Athena was a wise goddess with flashing eyes, who dressed in a white robe and a helmet of gold and had taken care of Odysseus through all the perils of his life. 'Come to me, my little goddess,' Harry Masters would say to Athena. Recognising the cue, she would run to him and be petted and have gifts bought for her. This was wonderful, to be so loved by such a wonderful man. She glowed. She felt beautiful, absorbing her father's charm and reflecting it back at him. The gifts came, on and off, although they could not afford it and although she often went to school in shamefully old clothes. 'You love your father, don't you?' he would say. 'You'll take care of your old man.'

That was when he was in a good mood. There were other times when he ignored her, or slapped her, or when she would wake to hear her mother being beaten. His good and bad moods were entirely unpredictable, but so was the rest of their life. Furniture she grew attached to disappeared overnight. Sometimes it re-appeared, but usually it was gone for good. Her father also disappeared and reappeared. When he came back from an absence, he would spoil Athena and she would feel loved, but the joy of it was accompanied by an air of suppressed fury that pervaded the house whenever he was home. It was a disembodied thing, this murderous fury. It was only years later that Athena realised that the anger had belonged to somebody. The fury had been felt by her mother, that silent and bitter woman who never shouted but who could fill the house with her feelings. Athena learned this skill from her mother. From her father, she learned how to fascinate.

They had moved house often, from one tight Adelaide suburb to another, staying one step ahead of eviction and debt collectors.

Always they moved further from the centre, towards the band of hills that marked the city's eastern limits. They never lived in the hills, that was only for the well-to-do. Rather, they lived on the plain below, where cheap new housing estates were eating up the market gardens. The hills had been quarried for stone and as they moved from suburb to suburb the white quarry scar shifted on the horizon. It was a reference point for Athena, until, as a result of protests from conservationists, it was painted over in grey-green with the idea that this would make it blend in, ridding the city of an eyesore. Athena could still find it, though, when she wanted to. She sought it out.

Whenever they moved, Athena had to start at a new school. Her strangeness, her funny name, her increasing size and her poverty marked her out for teasing. Once, faced with a new student in the middle of term, the teacher had not been able to find her a proper desk and sat her in a corner with a stool in front of her. A boy on the other side of the class was asked to make room under his lift-top desk for Athena's things. Every time there was a change of lesson she had to stand up and, with the whole class looking at her, go over to his desk and ask for her books. He would be chatting with one of his friends, or would already have something on top of the desk, and be unwilling to reorganise himself. Sometimes he refused to help her, or jeered at her for being new and badly dressed. She would walk back to her corner, scared of being punished for not having the right textbook, but more terrified still of remaining on her feet when the rest of the class had settled. After a week of this floating existence, she had diarrhoea in her pants as she pushed her bike up the hill towards home. She went to bed as soon as she got home.

'Are you ill?' her mother asked, and Athena did not know the right answer. She certainly did not feel well, but the problem was that she could no longer control herself. The chaos was getting inside.

The next day after school, she was followed by two boys as she pushed her bike up the hill.

'Did you shit yourself?' they said. She walked on, pushing her bike, her face impassive.

'Why do you wear such funny clothes?' She did not reply. 'Can't you talk?'

It went on for twenty minutes, all the way up the long, dusty road. She did not speed up or slow down. She walked at a measured pace, her eyes fixed on the quarry scar.

'Can't you talk? What's wrong with you? Don't you know how to use a toilet? Did you know you've got a big bum? A big arse? A big arse for Arse-ena.'

She walked on. It was easy, she thought. You did not have to mind them. You did not have to respond. Near the top of the hill, the boys grew frustrated at her lack of response. They walked closer to her, and touched her buttocks. Still she did not respond. Then one of them raised his school bag, full of books, and brought it crashing down on her head. The pain blinded her. Tears came to her eyes, but she did not look back. Clutching her handlebars, she kept walking. Then she was at the top of the hill, and in a delicious moment mounted her bike and sped down, leaving her persecutors behind. She was free and she was powerful, and from then on she was aloof and proud in the face of teasing. She took to walking home with the straps of her school bag around her fist, the buckle facing outwards. She thought of the punishment she could inflict if anyone attacked her.

As she grew older her impassiveness turned to poise, and in spite of her size she was popular with boys. She knew how to draw them in. She could generate sexual tension as well as the other sort. She could be . . . enigmatic.

Once, Athena had shown Jean photos of herself with a beehive hairdo and miniskirt, lolling impassively in the arms of a hulking man. She told Jean that the man had once been her fiancé.

'Why did you break it off?' Jean had asked.

Athena shrugged. 'He was a fuckwit.'

'Then why did you get engaged to him?'

'Because he was a good fuck.'

There was more to it than that, of course. True, he was no intellectual, but Athena had put herself out to enthral him. She had smiled and teased and been the most animated in any group. She laughed at his jokes. She eyed his body. His proposal was a victory, but once it was made, she grew bored. She dumped him.

Athena had become a nurse because it meant she could move out of home to nursing college. She quit that after only a year, without completing her training and in spite of the still-potent fascination of diagrams of the human body. She took a string of jobs. She was a secretary many times, and a waitress. She worked as an assistant in a pathology lab, and for the year before she moved to the farm she worked for a travel agent. Her intelligence and efficiency made her good at whatever she did, but she was not always good with people. Her conversation was designed to keep others on the back foot: she swerved between humour and aloofness with no warning. She would ask personal questions, flirt when it was not appropriate, or shock; she would not smile when social ease demanded it. Like her mother, she projected her mood and wrapped other people in her thoughts. Most often, her mood was angry. There would always be a few who were intrigued, even fascinated, by her but most of her colleagues avoided eye contact. They did what they could to be rid of her. For Athena the important thing was to remain potent and in control, even when that meant being preposterous.

To those who were fascinated by her, she could be extraordinarily generous. Jean was one of these people. Before Athena moved to the farm, she had rented a house in the inner suburbs of Adelaide. Most of the time she lived alone but every now and again, feeling guilty about the lack of economy, she would take in a housemate to share the rent. These arrangements were never happy for long and, when each housemate left, Athena would spend a weekend cleaning the house from top to bottom — not because she felt it was dirty, but because she wanted to make it her own again.

Jean had been closer and had lasted longer than any of the others, until Athena moved to Newera. Jean was eighteen compared to Athena's twenty-eight, and easily influenced. Athena lavished kindness upon her. With her queenly gait and impassive stare, her indifference, her shrugs and her stream of lovers, Athena was overwhelmingly impressive to Jean.

'You're wonderful,' she would say to Athena, as they cooked or washed up together, and Athena would turn away.

Athena propositioned men, and was rarely refused. She knew how to fill the air with sex, so they breathed it in. Once one of her men had eaten a meal she had prepared for him, then leaned back on the legs of his chair and said: 'That warms my heart, that does.' He looked up at her with shining eyes, and her heart softened towards him. She reached out a hand to stroke his thinning hair. He grabbed her arm and bit it, making munching noises, pretending to eat the flesh off her bones as though she was part of the meal. She kept smiling, but the softness had gone out of her heart.

Athena had all kinds of men — married, single, smart and dull. She had them almost on principle. This man had seen her as a fleshy, simple thing but in her stomach she knew that her spirit was feather-light and vulnerable.

Athena seized on aphorisms. The walls of the house were a source of constant exhortation. In her hallway she had a picture showing a child reaching for a branch, and the words said: 'The joy is in reaching, not in getting.' On the fridge there was a flower, with the words: 'The most admirable quality is restraint.' Jean assumed, wrongly, that this referred to some attempt on Athena's part to lose weight. In the living room there was a picture of a seagull against a cloudless sky, with the words: 'Fly with what you've got'. But the poster Athena carried in her mind was the one which hung on her bedroom door. It showed a butterfly, with the words: 'If you love something, let it go. If it comes back, it is yours. If it doesn't, it never was.'

One night when they were talking, Jean asked Athena how her men coped with her having other lovers, and how she handled their infidelities? Athena referred Jean to the poster on the door.

'If the love is real, you shouldn't need to hold on.'

Jean was not satisfied. It seemed silly to her. If the butterfly came back after you had let it go, were you then allowed to hold on to it? Or did you have to keep on letting it go, always hoping it would come back, in which case it was never really yours? Or could you only hold on to something if you did not really love it? She never suspected that at times, Athena would repeat the words to herself in desperation. Athena needed to know she was safe, that she was in control. Yet as soon as she won one of her power struggles, she lost interest. The men she fell hardest for were the ones who were immune to her methods, whose indifference matched her own facade, but whose hearts she believed were noble. They resembled the shining enigma, the unknowable and unconquered free spirit that the little girl had believed she saw in her father. Such men were a challenge she was quite unable to resist, and she drew them to her with joy and fury. These men, she could not let go.

VI

The truck blundered its way through the hot air. The land was not entirely flat but from behind the wheel, Athena could see so far that she fancied she could detect the curve of the earth. She was dreaming again — so calm, now that the baby was close.

The first thing you noticed about the dry, she thought, was the smell. When it was hot like this the air smelt of baked spice as though a fruit cake had recently been put in the oven. It was the scent of eucalypt and dust and straw. A better smell was when you watered the dryness. In the evenings when the sky was pink or red, Sam would be out in the paddock as the sprinklers came on. She would see him far away, and then he would come towards her, his shadow preceding him and the smell all around him. He would see her looking at him and say: 'What?' And she would say: 'What's what?' and he would shrug, and they would walk to the farmhouse together side by side, not touching, as the stones cast long purple shadows and the sky turned to grey.

Athena had met Sam at a car rally in the Adelaide Hills. She had been navigating for a team led by one of her boyfriends, and Sam was one of the drivers. He was tall with a creased face. At first she found him boring, with his silences and remoteness. Then, in the heat of the drive, she had watched him at the wheel. His driving was a matter of flick and catch, the car millimetres from disaster and at the same time completely under his control.

Talking to him was hard work. He answered her questions and laughed at her jokes, but gave no hint of what he was thinking. He was an electrician, he told her. His parents had made sure that he learned a trade. He was saving to buy a farm. He wanted to be his own boss, and get away from city living. She admired the courage of this, and the way it marked him out from men with more pedestrian ambitions. He didn't tell her, of course, about the time not so many weeks ago when he had found himself under one of the huge stamping machines at the Nissan car factory, fiddling with wires, and had been momentarily paralysed by the noise and the closeness. He wanted to get out, get away and be alone, but in his mind this was weakness, not strength.

Sam was the sort of man who would have named independence as one of the qualities he most liked in a woman, meaning that he did not want a woman who would ask very much of him. He never gave a compliment, and never seemed impressed by anything

Athena said or did, yet his eyes were full of animation. He listened to her in a way that left no doubt about his intelligence. His face reminded her of landscape. The lines around his eyes from the sun were like the creeks and gullies marked on a map, fanning out across his skin. She invited him to dinner.

When Athena told Sam about her unhappy childhood he was unsympathetic. He shrugged and said: 'I think you make a decision in life. Either you let these things bother you, or you don't.' He actually believed this to be true. To Athena, Sam's self-containment seemed like a promise of peace and constancy, and his remoteness looked like self-sufficiency. At the same time, being who she was, she wanted to break this down and work herself into his life, and so she searched for the crack that would let her inside. He was unconquered. He was exactly the sort of unknowable man she fell for.

Soon, Athena was in a fever of insecurity about Sam. Like a pigeon pecking at a button, she sought his approval. Of course, she could never admit that that was what she wanted. They were independent. That was part of the understanding between them. Neither needed the other. That was what they said. But Athena was anxious. She breathed in and tasted the sour breath of anxiety. She replayed their amicable conversations in her head, checking them for flaws or signs of slackening affection. In the middle of her day, she would think of him and breathe in, and taste the sour breath. She became obsessive. She would think: 'He didn't laugh at my joke this morning. He is bored. He will leave me.' Or, after a few days without contact, she would become absolutely convinced that he hated her. Most of all, she knew, he hated her seeking reassurance, and so with him she adopted a bluff and casual air. She would slap his bottom as he passed by or, when others were present, she would remark on how good he looked in her dressing gown. This was about power. It was almost sexual harassment. She was declaring her possession of him.

There were times, at work, and for the first few seconds after waking, when she was free of this sickness of anxiety. But the rest of the time it consumed her. Thoughts of him played and replayed in her mind. Sometimes she was weary of it all, and thought she was sick of him, but no sooner had the thought crystallised than the sour breath was there again. She had to reach out, first nudging, then pushing, finally slamming the thing between them. She could not trust it to be there. The more she slammed at it, the more she brought him under her control and the more he retreated from her.

A year after they began to sleep together, Sam moved to the Newera farm and she began to visit him at weekends.

The farmhouse was on top of a cliff, and from the verandah there was a view of the river and its big floodplain, and closer to the horizon, another loop of river, a hint of cliff and another loop. The garden was neglected — full of weeds and prickles. Athol pines, weird-looking trees so common and so hardy in the dry that most people assumed they were natives, cast scanty shade. In fact, Athena had been told, the trees had been introduced from Africa. They had no proper form and a littering habit. Their leaves were long spines, splaying in emaciated hands from drooping grey branches, and they bore tiny wooden nuts which, on the hottest days, could be heard cracking open. One weekend the drains at the farmhouse blocked up with their roots. Together, Sam and Athena worked for hours in the heat to dig up the pipe. When they finally uncovered it, they could see no sign of the roots. They stood in the sun's glare, gasping and looking in puzzlement at the pipe. Then Sam pounced. He had seen a tiny crack in the smooth white plastic. Growing into that crack was a hair-like root. He broke the pipe with his shovel. Inside was a mass of thirsty wood, all of it growing and expanding from the tiny filament that had worked its way through the fracture. It took them an hour to clear the pipe and repair it. Later, Athena thought of the tiny root and the vast water collection system which it had burgeoned. Water must have travelled back through that filament root at extraordinary speed, as though powered by a pump. Such dull-looking trees, and so cunning in their hunger. She liked to think of it.

Sam and Athena were wrong about each other. Each saw the other as strong. Sam thought Athena's aloofness was a guarantee that she would not make demands of him which he feared he might not be able to meet. Sam did not have the words to deal with emotions, and Athena, needing to control, could not afford to admit need. The rules of their game said that neither could acknowledge what was going on, or even that they cared enough to fight. It was agreed between them, for example, that each was free to have other lovers. For Sam, this was academic. He did not connect easily with people. But until she moved to Newera Athena's stream of men continued unabated. None of them affected the depth of her bond to Sam, or challenged the intensity of their battling.

Five months after Sam moved to Newera, Athena followed. Once she asked Sam why he had been willing to have her move in. The question was a crude tactic, and not one he was going to fall for.

'Because you wanted to,' he said.

It was true that she had made all the moves. She told him she loved the country, and the view from the farmhouse verandah. Scanning the local paper, she had seen and applied for a job with the Riverland Tourism Authority, promoting Newera. Her experience with the travel agency in Adelaide made her the best qualified of the few applicants and she got the job.

Jean visited her in the first month after she moved up. Sitting in the farmhouse, darkened against the summer heat, she watched Athena sew a padded picture frame in paisley cotton, her needle making precise, tight stitches.

'I've decided to have a child,' Athena said, without warning.

Jean gasped. 'That's great.' She hesitated. 'Sam must be pleased.'

'He doesn't know. I haven't told him.'

Two months later, Athena fell pregnant. She told Sam it was an accident. He was lying in front of her at the end of a long day, watching the evening news on television. She could see his face in profile. He was absorbed. It was a good moment.

'Sam, I've got something to say.'

His face flickered with irritation at the interruption. He was used to living alone.

'What?'

'I'm pregnant.'

His face went rigid. This was panic. She saw it as anger.

'It was an accident,' she said. 'I won't abort it. I want a child.'

Still his face was frozen. She got up and turned towards the kitchen, feeling in control.

'It will be my child,' she said. 'You won't have to have anything to do with it.' She looked over her shoulder at him. He was still frozen. She went out to put the kettle on.

Sam lay there trying to work out what to think. The weather map came and went. A game show began. Athena came back into the room. Sam was still speechless, frightened and confused but able to admit to neither. He felt incapable of getting up.

Athena said: 'My child. It won't . . . mean anything.'

'Okay,' he said.

'Okay?'

'Yes.'

But of course it did mean something. This was part of the paradoxical battle between them. By becoming a single mother, she reinforced her independent image. By having his child, she hoped to bind him to her.

By this time, Athena herself was not sure whether the pregnancy was accidental. She had spoken to Jean partly for the pleasure of shocking her. It was true she had not put her diaphragm in on the crucial night. Had she forgotten, or had she planned this child? She had stopped asking herself the question.

After only a few months in her new job Athena took maternity leave. Sam did not pamper her and she refused to admit any weakness because of her condition. She used the time to make herself indispensable on the farm. Nothing was said, but Sam could feel her moving closer to him. He was feeling smothered. He needed some air. He was beginning to struggle.

VII

Athena was passing a concrete dinosaur — a *Tyrannosaurus rex*. Once green, now bleached albino, it loomed over the road outside Renmark advertising a reptile farm. It was Athena's landmark. Just past it was the turn off to the Thomas' farm. The engine hissed as Athena struggled with the clutch and gearstick, turned off the main road and drove down the dirt track to the farmhouse.

Rosie Thomas was coming to meet her. When Rosie saw who was behind the wheel she broke into a trot, her mouth open. When the truck stopped she was already at the door, bobbing her grey head, her eyes full of concern.

'You *never* drove it yourself. I didn't think you would. And how long is it to go? Why on earth did he let you. Sam. Oh you never did. And so hot. So hot too.'

Rosie's legs were brown with the rough tan that comes from walking and working in the sun. She wore ankle socks with sandshoes, and a stiff, triangular skirt with a buttoned blouse. Her nails were cut to perfect half moons and she moved through the day with no urgency and no idleness. Her conversations were vague stabs at meaning. She repeated phrases, groped for words, then fell silent, always unable to capture quite what she wanted to say. Although Renmark was her nearest town, Rosie came from a Newera family, and remained for most purposes a member of Newera society. She drove over to the Newera Lutheran Church every Sunday, leaving her husband working on the farm. After the service she would stand outside the little white church talking to her friends and family, their conversations interrupted by the dust and noise of the semi-trailers. She was on the church committee responsible for writing the mottoes for the noticeboard outside the church. The night before they had met and decided on a new motto for the coming week: GOD GIVES ENOUGH FOR MAN'S NEED, BUT NOT FOR HIS GREED.

Rosie liked the mottoes, and she liked the committee, although she had never been able to make up a rhyme herself. She spent the meetings murmuring to herself 'God is good . . . God is everywhere . . . love, love . . . for the love of God,' but she could never get a rhyme or a witty idea, and so she grew used to applauding others.

Now she stood at the door of the truck, thin arms reaching up towards Athena's bulk as though, rather than see her climb down, she would lift and cradle her.

'You never did. You never did.'

Athena made a clumsy descent with her skirt, wet with sweat, clinging to her buttocks. The men came over with the tractor and began to unload the hay.

'You go and have a cuppa,' Don Thomas told her. 'I'll come and write you a cheque in a mo.'

Rosie and Athena walked down the track to the farmhouse, awkward in each other's company.

'Sam. How's Sam?' Rosie asked.

'Fine. Very busy.'

'He must be so pleased . . . the baby, I mean.'

Athena shrugged. 'I don't know. It's my baby really.'

There was a silence, then Rosie said: 'But he's your husband . . . your husband.'

'We're not married.'

Rosie's world shifted slightly. It had not occurred to her that they might not be married, and now she wasn't sure of the appropriate response. She felt pity, but knew this might offend. Athena frightened her a little. Words rushed to her mouth.

'Ah well. Well, when I had mine . . . the heat's what gets to you . . . I'd have never driven that . . . I mean Don would never have let me . . . well. You poor thing. You poor thing.'

As they reached the cool of the farmhouse, Athena said: 'In Africa the women work up until the moment it drops, then they carry right on working.'

'Africa.' Rosie put the kettle on the stove. 'Well. Africa. I don't know about . . . I saw a film once, of course. In Adelaide. Not so often now . . . so far . . . and the church . . . .' Her voice faded away.

'Have you travelled at all?' asked Athena.

'Not very far. Sydney once, ten years ago. That was the furthest. Beautiful, but you know . . . very strange,' she shook her head.

'Why strange?'

Rosie paused, teapot in her hand, and cocked her head as she tried to find the words. In Sydney she had seen the harbor and the sunset from the Manly Ferry and had been almost offended by the beauty of it all. It had felt so strange to return home, to the dry farm and the daily routine, with the dishes gathering dust in the rack and the tree roots growing into the drains. She had sniffed the salt and seen the bridge joining the two shores. So different from the fraught little villages on the Murray. All her life she and her God had occupied a place where everything was tenuous, and He was needed to help inhabit the silence. In Sydney, she had not known where to find herself, or Him. But she had words for none of this.

'Oh I don't know,' she said at last. 'Sydney. It's on the edge . . . the coast I mean. That harbor. I think I'm just a homebody. A biscuit?' and she reached to the shelf for the tin, her skirt lifting to show the nylon lace on her petticoat.

Don came in, gulped his tea and wrote Athena a cheque. When the women were alone again, Rosie came and sat down by Athena, her cup perched on her bony kneecap. She was feeling a sense of duty.

'You're not worried. I mean. You're not in trouble . . . I mean, not being married?'

'I don't want to be married,' Athena said.

'But the baby . . .'

'It will be loved,' said Athena, her eyes challenging Rosie to deny it.

'Oh yes. Well, he is the father. I suppose, he will have a . . . a . . . father's feeling.'

Athena could not resist. Rising from her chair and stretching, she said: 'Well, I guess he's the father, but really I'm not sure. I'd better be off. Thanks for the tea.'

She waddled towards the door, hand in the small of her back, while Rosie sat on the edge of her chair, mouth open and eyes filling with tears of confusion.

The truck was unloaded and only a few tangles of hay were left on the flat top. The fierceness had gone out of the sun now, but it was still hot. Athena was filling the radiator when Rosie came out of the house, moving like an awkward bird. She had put together a thermos of cool drink and some sandwiches for the return journey. Handing them to Athena, she said: 'Pop in anytime. I mean, if you want. We're always here. Pop in. And . . .' she paused. 'Come to church. That is, if you like. Come to church. It's . . . come to church. My dear. My dear.'

Athena felt mean.

The journey home was quicker thanks to the cooling of the air and the lack of a load. Athena only had to stop once to refill the radiator, and she reached Rosie's little church on the edge of the

Newera irrigation area just as the sun was setting. The minister was out by the board, changing the message. Only one word remained of last week's motto: DROWN.

By the time she came to the Big Orange, Athena couldn't see it because of the gathering gloom.

A strange car was parked in the farmhouse drive, but the house itself was in darkness. Athena walked in, snapping on lights and calling. Sam came to the bedroom door, and at first she thought he must have been sleeping. Then, bustling past him, she saw the rumpled bed and in it, a woman. For a moment she thought she was going to shout out loud, but she didn't. More than ever aware of her bulk, she walked out again. Sam, naked, stood aside to let her pass. Their eyes met, but both held their faces rigid. Athena went out to the kitchen and filled a saucepan to boil potatoes. Then she went out to sit on the verandah, feeling the early evening mosquitoes suck her blood, and the breeze on her strained stomach. After a while she heard the back door swing and the woman's car depart. The tail lights disappeared up the hill towards the highway and the back door swung again as Sam came back in. Athena waited for a while, then went in to cook chops for tea. Her face was haughty, and one hand was clutching her dress, wrinkling and clutching, wrinkling and clutching, working in the grime of her journey.

CHAPTER TWO

NEW ERA

I

The story of Chinny-kinnik, as recorded by Kingsford Laws, founder of New Era.

Chinny-kinnik was a giant who lived in a cave on the dry mallee plains to the south of the river valley. Chinny-kinnik was also a cannibal. Some of the river people who went to the plain to hunt or dig for yams never returned, and it was whispered in the camps that Chinny-kinnik had eaten them.

Soon, no yam-diggers or hunters would work the country on that side of the river. In summer, the river was surging and bloated. There were enough yabbies and fish to keep everyone well fed, but by late autumn it would dwindle to a stream, and the fear of Chinny-kinnik meant there was not enough food. The old people gathered to decide what should be done. Although they suspected

Chinny-kinnik, he was their relative and without proof they couldn't move against him. Two of Chinny-kinnik's uncles were among that summer's gathering of Ngawait, and the council decided it was up to them to determine whether the suspicions were justified and, if they were, to destroy Chinny-kinnik.

The next day the two men walked south until they lost sight of the river and could see only the plain, the sandhills and the mallee. They found fresh tracks leading into the scrub. Keeping downwind, they hid and after many hours they saw Chinny-kinnik and his two sons pass in front of them and disappear into a cave hidden in a dip in the sand and limestone.

The uncles decided to hunt up the means for a feast, and to invite Chinny-kinnik to share it with them in the hope that he would give himself away. They made camp near some wombat holes. At dusk, when the air was cooling and the animals came out to feed, the men crept up and placed big stones as far as they could reach down the burrows. When the wombats returned at dawn, the men trapped one in the mouth of the burrow and took it with them back to a place near Chinny-kinnik's cave, where they hid. When Chinny-kinnik appeared, the two men released the wombat and ran after it into the open, yelling aloud and throwing their spears. They killed it with a spear between the shoulders, then they greeted Chinny-kinnik with a show of surprise and told him they were going to cook the animal and that he was invited to the feast. Chinny-kinnik accepted, and showed them a place where they could find cooking stones. The men dug a hole, lined it with the stones and lit a fire on top of them. They used the last of their water to mix clay to a paste, and this they rubbed on the fur of the wombat, until the whole animal was covered in plaster. When the stones were glowing, the wombat was wrapped in mallee leaves and grass and buried in the hole.

At dusk the men saw Chinny-kinnik coming towards their camp. The giant was outlined against the evening sky, and the men were frightened. Controlling their terror, they opened the oven and placed the wombat on bark. They broke the clay shell, and the animal's hair came away with it. The smell of cooking made Chinny-kinnik hungry. He feasted with the two men and, when his stomach was full, he relaxed and became merry, but his uncles were worried. They still had no evidence against Chinny-kinnik, and they could not kill a relative for no reason.

They asked him to sing, thinking that since most songs were about hunting exploits he might give himself away, but when Chinny-kinnik sang, his voice was so loud that it deafened them and they couldn't hear the words.

Chinny-kinnik lay down to sleep by the fire. The two men pretended to do the same, but didn't close their eyes. In the morning, they asked Chinny-kinnik to give them some meat for the homeward journey although in fact they had brought plenty of supplies. Chinny-kinnik went away to his cave and brought back meat. The two men saw it was part of two human legs. Struggling to control their fear and retching, they pretended to munch on the limbs, but they didn't eat the meat. Then they broke their camp and pretended to make off. Instead, they doubled back and hid in the bush, where they gathered huge piles of firewood and dry sticks.

When the sun set, a cold wind came from the south, but still they waited. Finally, Chinny-kinnik came towards his cave, shivering and calling to his sons for fire. After he had gone in, the two men quietly carried the dry grass and bushes to the entrance and set it alight with a firestick.

The men heard cries of terror, and immediately the two boys they had seen with Chinny-kinnik the morning before came to the entrance. The men pulled them through the burning brush to safety. Then the entrance was closed with logs, and more wood was thrown on the fire, so that a great sheet of flame rose out of the pit.

The earth shook with the struggles of the giant below, and his thunder-like voice made it difficult to speak. Turning to one of the two boys, the men said: 'Aren't you glad we pulled you out and killed your father, who killed and ate his people and probably your mother?' But the boys answered that they were not pleased, and when they grew older they would do as their father had done, for he had taught them all they knew.

So the uncles of Chinny-kinnik caught the two boys, their nephew's sons, and threw them into the fire.

The uncles waited until Chinny-kinnik's raging had stopped, and they were certain that he was dead, then returned to the river and told the Ngawait what they had done. There was a great celebration and, when the river dropped that winter, the people were able to hunt on the plains again.

II

The Newera that Athena knew had as its centre a sloping triangle of three main roads, their pavements dotted with large fibreglass rubbish bins, sponsored by Rotary and made to look like oranges. The pub, an old building of local stone, stood at the lowest corner of the triangle, buttressed on one side with a modern red-brick bottle shop and on the other by a two-storey block of motel units with faded doors, the windows blocked with noisy air-conditioners that leaked cold water over the pavement in summer.

Further down the hill ran the road to the ferry. Newera had never been big enough to justify a bridge. Cars and trucks drove on and were winched across the river. Bernie McLachlan was one of the ferrymen, working the night-shift by choice. When things were quiet, he slept in a little hut, barely big enough to take his single bed. Motorists could summon him by pressing a bell, and he would rise, stretch, go out into the blackness, sometimes pee, then half asleep drive the creaking ferry across the river, smelling grease and dark river smells, sometimes seeing a fish splash in the headlights of the cars.

Sometimes Bernie couldn't sleep, and would lie awake on the narrow bed and dream of ways to make his life less monotonous. Since he was not a brave or an imaginative man, his dreams came down to ways of spending money. Bernie bought gadgets. The year before, he had bought a model radio-controlled car and taken it to the pub, where he raced it around the bar stools and tripped up waitresses until the excitement faded and his mates told him to can the noise. Bernie had two expensive cameras that he never used. He had been the first person in Newera to own a compact disc player, and he had ordered an iron which, according to the advertisements, could take the creases out of your pants without the need for an ironing board. Bernie's credit cards were always overdrawn and in arrears. He spent his own money, and the money earned by his wife, but he left the worry over that to her. When the sun rose, Bernie would go home, sleep some more, then wake in time to get to the pub when it opened.

Across the road from the pub was the supermarket and next to it, the butcher's and the baker's and the TAB. Opposite these was the old Mechanics' Institute building, built after the First World War, now closed for most of the year. The Institute was the home of the Riverland Choral Society, an amateur group including most of the town's prominent citizens, which put on one performance a year, usually something from Gilbert and Sullivan. Last year it had been *The Mikado*. Yum Yum was played by the Mayor's wife, Allison Neil, and Alan Neil himself was the Lord High Executioner. The group practised for months, but on opening night the members of the chorus line had an attack of nerves and lost control of their fans, clicking them open and shut so disastrously out of time that Athena got the giggles and had to leave the hall.

Next to the Institute was a tiny craft shop run by volunteers — the same women who made the goods. The shop was full of the scent of rose petals, torn from a hundred cossetted gardens, mixed with spice and oil then sold for a dollar a jar. Streaky paintings of trees, the river, tumble-down homesteads and lost kittens hung on the walls. There were rows of pickles and jams: quince jelly, satsuma plum jam, guava and apple jam, fig jam with almonds, three-fruit marmalade, lemon butter, pickled carrots with mint, pickled watermelon rind, pickled cucumber chips, capsicum and mint jelly and tomato relish, all in re-used jars with cellophane lids, identified by labels written in the spidery copperplate taught at the Newera Primary School two generations before. There was jewellery made from gum nuts and horseshoe nails, and then the crocheted and knitted and sewn things: woollen rugs and dresses for babies and slings intended to hold three toilet rolls, sewn out of denim and decorated with sprigs of lavender. There were also dainty padded photo frames, made with paisley cotton, polystyrene padding and nylon lace. These were made by Athena. She sewed them for relaxation, and sold them for between five and ten dollars apiece. The shop kept five per cent.

At the top of the road, marking the second corner of the triangle, was a small green park. It was dominated by what looked like a wall of metal the size of a small house, with pipes attached and a large wheel at one end. This was the pump which had first been used to lift the water into the irrigation channels. Once glossy green, it was now dull and speckled with rust. On a plate at one end the word 'Worthington' appeared in letters of raised metal. It had once been a word to conjure with, representing the best of Victorian engineering. The pump had been shipped from England then towed up the river on a barge. Days had been spent preparing the landing site with logs so it could be rolled ashore, but when the steamer arrived the captain said the ground was too soft and he unloaded the pump half a mile upstream. It had taken a week for half the settlers and a horse to move it back to its place by the river, where it had stayed until taken out of service and moved to the park. Now drinking straws and paper bags crammed the holes where the water pipes had once been, and the peeling paint was scratched with the initials of louts and lovers. On the side facing away from the street, someone had spray-painted the unintentionally appropriate word 'SUCKS'.

At the highest corner of the triangle was a big roundabout, the meeting point for the main roads into town. Standing here, one could glimpse the river through the forest of television aerials necessary for good reception on this side of the Adelaide Hills. Overlooking the roundabout was a modern brick building, which housed all levels of government. The police station was at one end and the council offices were in the middle. Athena's office was in the middle of the second arm. Next to her was the state Department of Engineering and Water Supply, and on the other side, an office that was usually vacant, but which was used by the single official of the Department of Social Security, who spent one day a fortnight in each of the Riverland towns.

Athena's office had a view of the roundabout, which was entirely covered in grass. At noon, when the heat could be so fierce it took an effort of will to step out into it, sprinklers popped up and sent out shattered arcs of water over the green. The excess ran off and across the road, making its way in glistening ropes down the gutters, flowing freely and to waste past the shops, the orange-shaped dustbins, the community hall and the pub, under the parching sun.

When Jean first came to visit Athena on the farm, she saw there were two cold-water taps in the kitchen. Athena explained that one of these was for rainwater, which you could drink, and the other for river water. Sam had his own pump at the foot of the cliff, and the water it lifted supplied both house and sprinklers. No one drank the river water. It had, after all, already drained and watered a fifth of the continent.

'That's awful,' Jean said.

'Why?'

'What would happen if it didn't rain? What would you drink?'

Athena shrugged. 'Well, it doesn't rain, much.'

They were sitting on the verandah of the farmhouse, the river sweeping in indolent curves in front of them. Near the horizon to the east, on the rise of a sandhill, they could see a patch of deep colour, a green circle where oranges and grapes were grown with water pumped through the network of pipes that connected the land to the river.

'If you don't water it, it don't grow,' said Athena.

As they watched, the sprinklers were turned on, and the orchards disappeared under plumes of water.

In the early days of colonisation, it had been said that the land to the east of the Adelaide Hills should not be settled. The mallee was said to be too resistant to clearing, the rainfall insufficient to support agriculture and the land itself too fragile to bear up to habitation. Irrigation had changed all that. It had seemed a blessing, and the water that surged through the channels and pipes was holy water, bringing civilisation to the wilderness. But now, just as their grip on the land seemed firmest, the water was turning against the Riverlanders.

Months after Jean's visit, when Athena drove the load of lucerne hay up the river, she noticed the Big Orange poking out of the orchards where no oranges used to grow, and the little white church by the side of the road, and the *Tyrannosaurus rex* where no such dinosaur had ever wandered. She noticed the greens of irrigation advancing and receding. But there were some things she couldn't see. Strange things, that were happening underground.

There had always been water hidden underneath the great bowl of land drained by the Murray. In some places, bores could be sunk and it would spurt to the surface. This groundwater had its own flows. It seeped across the continent from east to west, draining, like the above-ground watercourses, to the Murray. In the east the groundwater was sweet enough to drink, but as it flowed it took up the salts in the earth and by the time it reached the apparently waterless wastes of the Mallee it was saltier than the sea.

Before the coming of the Europeans, the water lay far beneath the surface. The mallee trees used up most of the rain before it could seep through to the aquifers, and the salt water that drained from the aquifers to the river was flushed each spring to the sea. Then the trees were cleared, and the Murray harnessed with locks and weirs to regulate its flow. On the land, rain seeped past the shallow-rooted European crops. Slowly at first, then more rapidly, the underground water began to rise. From twenty-five metres down, it rose to within a few metres of the surface, and with it came the salt that had lain in the ground since the continent was created. When the underground water came within two metres of daylight, trees began to die and crops grew more thinly, or not at all. The soil looked strangely greasy, and the leaves thinned on the trees.

In the mallee to the south of the highway that ran past Sam's farm there were acne-like scars in the dips between the sand dunes where nothing would grow except clumps of purple saltbush. There were desert towns where the cellars of the hotels were awash, and where mechanics could not use their garage inspection pits.

Irrigation made the problem worse. Much of the water that was poured on the land to sustain the orchards seeped into the aquifers, raising the water table even higher, so that now each irrigation area rested on a great, invisible water mound. The hydrologists in the salinity bureaucracies had drawn contour maps of this underground waterscape, and the lines gathered tightly around the tense little river towns. The Big Orange rested above the peak of the

Newera water mound, and where Athena had driven her load of hay past it and out into the dry, the water level sank, only to rise again under the dinosaur, and sink again where the road headed back into the dry.

On the stretch of cliffs between the farm and the little white church, the underground watercourses converged. For millions of years the salty flows had crept their way here, to these pink sandhills and golden cliffs, and seeped through the limestone far below the murky surface of the river. This was a natural process, but now it added to the salt that came downstream, from the rising tide under Victoria and New South Wales.

Within government departments, whole bureaucratic careers were being built on the search for solutions to salinity. The Murray-Darling basin, food bowl for the continent, was threatened. In a generation, if nothing was done, half the land within it would be laid waste.

On Athena's journey, the sky and the horizon were hot and quiet, seemingly immutable. Yet underground, was the inland sea that the explorers had searched for.

The land was not immutable, nor mute, nor indifferent. Underneath the green geometries of the Riverland, the tide was rising.

III

Lying on her back in the Newera Hospital, Athena was drugged and gasping. She had asked for pain relief early, although she had thought she would need nothing. As a trainee nurse, she had attended several labors and more recently had been to classes in the Newera Community Centre, where she had lain on a prickly green carpet and been taught to breathe in ways that were meant to control the pain. Yet she had been totally unprepared for the agony of the contractions, and now she was slipping between dreams and reality. The pethidine had not taken away the pain, but separated it from her, so now it was a disembodied thing, kicking at doors and knocking at windows, trying to get back inside. Athena could hear and feel it raging, but inside she felt calm and rational. She was chairing a meeting in a hall besieged by the pain. Some people wanted to panic but she was keeping them calm, although from time to time the words of the speakers were drowned out by the noise of the beast outside. When this happened, Athena and the others would push heavy items against the door, then wait for the noise to subside.

'How long is this likely to go on?' said one of the voices in her head.

She replied: 'The cervix has dilated. We have entered the second stage of labor.'

'And how does all this look to Sam?' the first speaker asked.

Sam was there. She had asked him to be at the birth, and he had come. His eyes swam above the debate, green and alert. She knew he could not hear what she could hear. He could see only her, clad in a starched linen gown that didn't even cover her backside (they had had none in her size). He would see her legs apart, eyes glazed, and her body carrying on without her. He wouldn't realise that inside, she was handling things in a totally capable fashion.

'Sam's eyes. There they are. And his hand touching our hand,' said one of the speakers inside her head. 'What is behind those eyes?'

'He looks concerned.'

'Or perhaps only amused. The crinkling of those lines around his eyes. It could be either.'

'Does he really care, or is he thinking of Dawn. The slim-line Dawn?'

The slim-line Dawn. The words caused a pause in the debate.

In the silence the pain attacked and all hands were needed to block the doors against it.

'Push, push,' said the pain, or was it the nurse? 'Now breathe. Steady.'

And above the meeting room which, strangely, had no roof, floated the green eyes of Sam.

'We're okay. We're okay,' Athena assured the meeting.

'But what's he thinking?'

'Not of her. Not of Dawn. Not now. He doesn't really love her.'

'Yes, but she is slim and sexy. She makes him feel good. All we do is criticise him. He doesn't even talk to us.'

'How long since we talked properly?'

'We may be going to lose him.'

'No.'

'No.'

'No.'

'There are his eyes again,' said Athena, trying to bring the debate back under control. 'And here is his hand in mine, holding tight. He is with us.' And over the din that the pain was making, Athena heard the thin woeful wail of love. It was trying to get in too, pushing past the beast.

Athena closed her eyes. 'Push, push,' she told the meeting, and they all ran to the door and pushed against it.

'Push, push,' said the nurse.

'We're doing it,' said Athena, crossly, and she felt Sam's hand tighten on hers.

'It doesn't matter now,' said Athena. 'We just have to concentrate on getting this done, then we'll work out what to do.'

Sam saw her close her eyes and set her jaw. He squeezed her hand, wondering what else he was meant to do, not knowing what to say.

Sam was not in the habit of examining his emotions. This sort of thing — birth — weighed him down, made him feel inadequate. When it came to the emotional world, he barely had the vocabulary. In his home, such things had not been talked about. No one knew what anyone else was feeling, or whether they felt at all.

As a child, he had played with the little girls next door, making fairy houses out of gum nuts and twigs, and telling stories about their residents. Sam was the best storyteller, with long tales of journeys and battles that took in all the shrubs and litter of the back yard. The girls welcomed him, but his father didn't like it. 'You're getting to be a sissy,' he said, and ordered Sam to stay at home. The next day, Sam's father found him with the girls again, playing fairy games. He chased him home and in full view of the neighbours, beat him with his belt. The next day Sam was too ill to go to school. He didn't go back to the little girls' house. Instead his father began to take him fishing and camping at the weekends. Sometimes it was just the two of them, but more often Sam's father brought his mates. The little boy spent hours being ignored, struggling to impress, and to speak and act with the taciturn toughness of the men. He wanted to be capable, like them, and independent, like them. When they did speak to him, or when his father ruffled his hair or playfully wrestled with him, Sam felt himself expand with inward joy. So he learned to be a manly man.

The things of the imagination were pushed away. He learned a trade, as was expected, and when, five years later, the girls from next door walked past the house his father nudged him violently in the ribs.

'They're orright. Waddya reckon?'

Sam took another sip of beer and looked at the girls. They had grown breasts and bottoms.

'Yeah,' he said. 'Orright.'

People called him a free spirit, which pleased him. He liked himself best when he was alone and capable. Being with people, particularly with Athena, required reflection. When she asked him what he was thinking, he didn't know how to reply. His thoughts flew away the minute he turned to look at them and in any case he could think of no way to express them that was . . . proper.

Now he was helpless. Why were fathers expected to be at births? He didn't belong here. It should be left to women, and people who knew what they were doing. Another, deeper part of him thought: I should be doing more. Feeling more. She's having my son.

'All right, love?' the nurse said to him. 'She's doing fine. Shouldn't be too much longer now.'

Athena bellowed and screwed up her face, squeezing his hand so that he feared for his fingers.

'What am I meant to do?' he thought. 'What am I meant to feel?' He wanted to say all sorts of things to her, including, surprisingly, that he was sorry.

A lot had happened in the six weeks since Athena had walked in on him and Dawn. Had Athena challenged him during that time, he would have argued, with perfect logic, that there was no reason why he should not be with Dawn, since Athena had had other men, and since theirs was an open relationship. But Athena had not argued with him about it. She was too smart. She seemed to understand the rules better than he did. Sam was always on the back foot.

Sam had met Dawn at the Newera pub when he dropped in one afternoon for a quick beer after chores in town. The lunch hour had passed, and the public bar was almost empty. Bernie McLachlan the ferryman was there as usual. His white hairy legs were wrapped around the bar stool, his beer belly was falling like a tear-drop over his belt and one elbow rested on the soggy bar towel with its design of boomerang-throwing Aborigines. Bernie was chatting to a woman, but he called Sam over as soon as he walked in.

'Gidday mate. A beer for my mate Sam, please love. Come over here, you bastard. Meet Dawn.'

Women were not normally seen in the public bar of the Newera Hotel, unless they were with a man. Even then, they were usually either passers-by from the city, or belonged to one of the fruit-pickers' gangs, in which women kept their place only by being as rough as the men. Local women drank in the lounge, taking their menfolk with them.

Bernie was clearly relieved that Sam had arrived. Although Bernie was always the first to leer at the barmaid's breasts or speculate on the sexual habits of his fellow drinkers, women made him nervous, and everything about Dawn suggested availability: her clothes (a fluffy pink jumper and leather pants), her presence in the bar, her posture, her air of watchful relaxation. With Sam there the pressure was off. Bernie could relax back into his normal role of clown. Dawn smiled at Sam, narrowing her eyes and drawing on her cigarette. Her hair was streaky blonde and cropped so it skimmed her shoulders.

'This is a bloke you ought to meet, Dawn,' Bernie said, as fresh glasses of beer were placed on the silhouetted Aborigines. 'Got his own farm.' Bernie turned to Sam. 'Dawn's new in town. Just moved into Sultana Street.'

That said a lot. Sultana Street was the new Housing Trust area, where single mothers, battered wives and families down on their luck were encouraged to move, with the idea that country towns offered a better life than the city.

Dawn blew out smoke. 'I thought farms kept a man poor,' she said. 'That's what I've been told.'

'Too true.'

'Not very eligible then, are you?'

'Guess not.'

She smiled at him.

'Reckon you could make him reconsider,' said Bernie. He was enjoying himself. Dawn and Sam both looked away.

'How long since you moved up?' Sam asked her, feeling the need to break the silence.

'Couple of months. Don't know anyone yet.'

'Lonely,' said Bernie, smiling.

'Aw yeah. I cope. My little boy . . .'

'Sam's not local either, you know.'

'Yeah?'

They compared notes on the suburbs they had lived in, and their reasons for leaving the city, then Sam fell silent while Bernie and Dawn kept the banter going, with him as the audience.

After an hour, Dawn got up, pulled at the zip of her pants, which had ridden halfway down, and said she had to go and pick up her son from school.

'You should pop round some time. Lunch tomorrow, d'ya think?' She was talking to them both, but it was clear that she meant Sam.

Bernie gave Sam a violent nudge, not bothering to conceal the gesture from Dawn. To his surprise, Sam found himself nodding in agreement. Dawn grabbed a beer mat and wrote her address down on it.

After she had left, Bernie said: 'I reckon you're in there, mate, you lucky bugger.'

'Yeah,' Sam said. 'I reckon I am.'

The next day he had gone to lunch, and then to bed with Dawn. It was all quite predictable. He had been relieved to slip so easily into a relationship that Athena knew nothing about, and over which she had no control. He didn't tell her about it, nor did he do anything to conceal it from her. He would leave the farmhouse in the evenings with no explanation, saying only that he was going into the town. The smell of grog on him when he returned led her to believe he went to the pub. Dawn knew about Athena, but accepted without question his assurance that their relationship was an open one, so Sam had no reason to stop and think about his own motivation, let alone hers. In a detached sort of way he supposed that she was lonely.

Then came the night when Athena had found them together. He expected a fight, waited for the storm to break. Dimly he thought there would be some sort of resolution. He had heard the truck pull up and the banging of the screen door and the calling of his name, and felt a rush of fear and excitement that far surpassed the mechanical sexual thrills of a few moments before.

Later, he and Athena had sat together over dry chops and overcooked potatoes.

'Pass the chutney,' he said.

Athena passed the jar with its black, sticky lid. 'Who is she?'

'Dawn. Dawn Bingham. Single mum. Lives in the Housing Trust estate.'

'How long have you known her?'

Sam squinted at the ceiling, jaws working over the meat and his mind numbing itself in preparation for the argument he was certain they were about to have.

''Bout two months.'

'You might have told me she was going to be here.'

'I didn't know. She just dropped in after you'd gone.'

Of course, he could have got rid of her before Athena's return, but he had not done so.

'You must bring her over,' Athena said. 'And introduce us properly.'

He looked up at her. He hadn't expected this. 'Okay,' Suddenly the dry chops felt like lead in his stomach.

He would not have introduced Athena and Dawn had he been left to himself but Athena took matters into her own hands. She invited Dawn to drop in while her son was at school. This was very like Athena. She wanted Dawn brought into her orbit, where she could see and assess her; where the other woman could be controlled and defeated.

For the first two visits, the women got on well. Athena extended herself to make Dawn feel comfortable. She invited her to drop in any time. Dawn thought they might even become friends. She needed friends.

This did not last long. On the third visit, Athena treated Dawn as an honoured guest. The coffee mugs were replaced with the best china. Dawn was quite unable to feel at home.

After that, whenever Dawn turned up, Athena would begin to do housework. She lumbered around with her swollen ankles and enormous belly. Carpets would be lifted from under Dawn's feet and the dust beaten out of them and into her face. Sam escaped outdoors. Left alone, Dawn offered to help.

'You'll tire yourself out, in your condition,' she said. 'I know what it's like, with no one to help.' Her offers were always refused.

Once, seeing Athena drag the vacuum cleaner from its place in the laundry, Dawn seized it from her and said: 'Let me help with this, at least.' She was halfway through doing the living-room floor, listening with satisfaction to the dust ping its way up the vacuum cleaner pipe, when suddenly it stopped working. Athena had pulled out the plug, and was standing holding the cord. Dawn's mouth was open, but when she saw Athena's face she fell silent. Without a word, Athena turned and put the plug for the iron into the socket where the vacuum cleaner had been. With a screech of metal, she set up the ironing board and began to shake and reorder a pile of clothes. Standing marooned on the carpet, clutching the powerless vacuum cleaner, Dawn felt herself defeated.

That evening, after Dawn had gone, Athena sat in her armchair, feet up, making neat even stitches in paisley material.

'I'm not happy, Sam,' she said.

He looked up at her from where he lay sprawling on the floor.

'I'm not happy,' she repeated, putting down her sewing.

'I know you're not happy.'

'I don't want Dawn here so much,' she said. 'This is my home too. She gets on my nerves.'

'It's my home too,' he said, sounding like her echo. 'And you invited her.'

'She pokes around my stuff. She wants to move in.'

'No she doesn't.'

'What do you think she's after, then? Why do you think she comes around, hangs around you?'

He was silent. He felt insulted. It didn't occur to him to say: 'Obviously, she likes me.' He shrugged. 'Okay, I'll see her at her place.'

'Thank you.'

Sam was left with the feeling that he was losing in a game played by rules he couldn't understand.

Athena had picked up her sewing again, and they had passed the rest of the evening in silence until, at about eleven o'clock, she had felt the first contractions. Her waters had broken on the way to the hospital, and now she was pushing and kicking and screaming, and Sam didn't know that she was holding the meeting to order, and keeping love and pain outside the doors.

'Push, push,' said the doctor. Sam saw the red head emerging. The face was washed in blood and mucus and screwed up in an expression of fury and disdain.

Athena heard the pain at the doors. This time, the barricades were breaking and the meeting was in disarray. 'Order, order,' called Athena, but her voice was drowned out. 'Order, order.' But the pain had eaten the speakers, and now it was heading for her. She braced herself against the beast's onslaught, but then, suddenly, taking her by surprise was a smaller, sharper beast, a tearing pain, a screaming thing. It came for her. It grabbed her and opened her up, then, suddenly, it dropped her.

'Its all right,' she told the remains of the meeting. 'Its all right. It's over.'

Then she saw the green eyes of Sam floating over the ruins, and heard his voice saying: 'Oh Jesus. Oh Jesus.'

'He's going to cry,' she thought.

The baby was laid upon her chest. It took her by surprise. It moved wetly against her, and she stopped trying to chair the meeting and panted with the shock of it.

'My God,' she said, lifting her hand to touch the baby on the back. 'What have I done?'

'You've had a beautiful little girl,' the nurse said. 'And the placenta's just coming nicely.'

The baby cried. Sam and Athena had not even discussed a name.

IV

Most people assumed that the name 'Newera' had come from an Aboriginal word. Visitors who called in at the tourism information centre often asked Athena for a translation, but she had to disappoint them. The town's name originally had been two words — New Era — but now the locals pronounced it as though it was 'Nearer', with only a faint slurred suggestion of the 'w' in the middle.

When she first learned about the name's origins, Athena was surprised that it had been so quickly corrupted, its meaning so totally lost. Even some of the locals assumed the town's name was Aboriginal, yet it was only a few years since the last of the original pioneers who had named the place had died.

Land had been an abstract to the New Era settlers. They chose the name at a rowdy meeting in Adelaide in 1893. South Australia was in deep depression, and land was at the centre of every political debate. The unemployed marched under black flags, chanting:

Oh government hear our petition
Find work for the strong willing hand.
Our dearest and greatest ambition
Is to settle and cultivate land.

But these people hadn't seen the inland. They hadn't seen the plain sweeping away in all directions, or the alien river. They hadn't touched the hot red sand, or wrestled the mallee roots that gripped the soil like claws. None of the eighty people at the meeting had any experience of agriculture. Most had never sown a seed. Yet they had come to believe that ownership of soil was the key to happiness.

For these people, the name New Era very quickly had come to sound like a bad joke. It could not be spoken without irony. How much of a relief it had been to lose the origins, to run the words together and speak them out of the side of the mouth, disowning the foolish hopes that had led the dispossessed up the river and into the wilderness.

The man credited with founding New Era was Kingsford Laws, a young lawyer who had been born in the closest thing Adelaide had to an establishment family; rich enough to set him up in his own practice. The good things of life had come easily to Laws, and as a result he didn't value them. He was drawn to the working class — another abstract concept — and what he imagined as their noble, manly qualities. Phrases like 'human happiness' flowed easily off his tongue. When he was twenty-five, Laws met the land reformer William Lane and was swept away by the idea of a New Australia beyond the colony's shores.

Two hundred South Australians, including some of its most prominent citizens, were planning to leave Port Adelaide for Paraguay, where land had been granted for the founding of a Utopia. Laws began to write for new reformist newspaper, the *Voice*, urging people to abandon 'this benighted place, with all its laws to protect the privileged' and sail to Paraguay. There would be no inequality. Settlers would give all they owned, live in communal village settlements and work for the common good. Happiness lay not in the interior, but outside, away from Australia's shores.

A few days before he was to sail, Laws' plans changed. The government altered the Crown Lands Act to allow groups of thirty or more people to form village associations and settle on Crown land. The settlements were to be run on 'communistic' lines — the leaders elected and all property held in common.

In his mind's eye, Laws fancied the inland (which he had never seen) as a vast, fertile plain where the downtrodden would become cheerful yeomen, their own masters, independent and loving. He imagined the village he would create, and the perfect blend of the intellectual and manual that would fill the working man's life. He would be a benefactor, a fatherly figure, a leader of men. The land was a blank page, waiting for him to write on it.

The Murray was the natural destination for the first village settlers. Irrigation engineers had already conjured the garden cities of Mildura and Renmark out of the desert, and there seemed no reason why the same miracle should not be repeated. Within days of the law changing, people were huddled on paddle-steamers, making their way up the Murray to form Waikerie, Lyrup and Moorook.

Laws published an article calling those interested in 'the highest ideals to which man can aspire' to come to a public meeting where a new village settlement association would be formed. The meeting was packed, the mood close to hysteria. Many signed up that night, willing to leave as soon as necessary. Most of them had nothing to lose, and a fifty-pound government advance to gain. The name was chosen by a show of hands. 'New Era' won narrowly over 'Jerusalem' and 'Utopia'.

At seven in the morning on a bright autumn day, the eighty settlers and their families gathered at the Adelaide railway station.

The trip to Morgan took all day. As dusk settled, the settlers huddled in the station house and took tea and damper provided by the townsfolk, then transferred their goods to the other side of the wharf and on to the paddle-steamer *Virgin*. It was a cloudy night, too dark for the settlers to see anything but vague shadows of trees on the banks. They reached New Era at three o'clock in the morning, just as it came on to rain. When the sun rose, they could see the raggedy trees, the ants already making their way into their provisions, and the blank, endless sky. It was cold and lonely. The men rigged up shelters out of saplings and canvas. The women built fires. Everyone tried not to cry. Even the frisky Laws, who walked around slapping shoulders and shouting encouragement, felt the first shadow of doubt.

In the early months, he led regular groups which met near the river to read to each other from the works of Marx, Ruskin and Carlysle. Then spring came, and the mosquitoes and the strangeness of the night drove the readers inside. In summer they were too exhausted with the heat to want to read and in the New Year Laws abandoned the groups.

By then, there were no illusions. The land was hostile. One mallee tree could take ten men all day to shift. People fainted in the heat. Children grew too sick to brush away the flies that crawled in their eyes. Winter came. Crops were sown, most of them only to be ruined when the river rose with the first flood of spring. Money was earned cutting wood for the paddle-steamers. The riverbank was soon stripped of its red gums, leaving only the tenacious, ugly scrub on the plain. That was cleared with axes and shovels, and slowly the hovels were replaced with pine houses, the gaps between the logs stopped with a paste of mud and reeds, which was renewed after the rains.

Laws was sacked as chairman in autumn — blamed by everyone. It was a secret relief to him, but he left the settlement in a huff. He couldn't return to Adelaide immediately. Dignity demanded an interval. He moved out into the bush where he grew vegetables and caught rabbits, and began to study the local Aborigines, sending artifacts and tales of their doings back to the newly established South Australian museum.

> *These are noble people,* [he wrote to the curator], *whose passing can only be regretted and recorded as well as might be. Surely these children of nature are the happiest beings, living in a natural communism which it is beyond us to attain, at peace with nature and each other. I count myself fortunate to be in a position to assist your institution.*

Laws befriended Thomas Pelican Short, an old man from the mission downstream. He gave Short food and a little money in return for his reciting the old legends, and making boomerangs, spears, bark canoes and waddies, which Laws sent on the paddle-steamer to the museum.

Settlers were leaving New Era daily. Those who remained argued among themselves. Work was constantly interrupted by the ringing of a bell which signalled the need for a meeting. Chairmen were sacked, reinstated and sacked again within weeks. One escaped a beating at the hands of the settlers by jumping through the window of the meeting hall. He landed on a pregnant woman, who miscarried as a result. He left for Morgan at dawn, and was never heard of again.

Ten years after it began, the government decided the communal system should be abandoned. The land was divided into ten-acre blocks and given to the remaining settlers.

New Era struggled on into the new century and economic recovery. After World War I the population swelled with soldiers, some of them straight off the troopship, who came to settle on parcels of land just big enough to ensure continued poverty. These people and their children had no idea what the town's name had originally meant. By then it was inconceivable that Newera had ever been a place of hope.

In the early 1960s Kingsford Laws died. He had long since retired to Adelaide to take up his inheritance and a prestigious position as patron of the museum. His executors found among his possessions a copy of *Das Kapital*. The first twenty pages, so often read aloud on the banks of the Murray, were well thumbed, but the rest had not even been cut.

Now Kingsford Laws' portrait hung in the council chambers at Newera. Athena gazed up at it on her first day at work, when she was being shown around by the Mayor, Alan Neil. Laws looked, she thought, like a thinner version of Colonel Sanders from the Kentucky Fried Chicken packs.

'Our founding father,' Alan Neil told her. 'I met him once, when I was a little kid.' He paused. 'A wonderful old man. So wise. The real pioneering spirit.'

Although its history was so short, Newera's collective memory was poor, or rather, selective. In New Era hope had not died hard. It died easily. People took root, and the economics of water and fruit were established, but ideas withered.

V

In the first hours of its life, Athena watched her baby sleep. Its lips moved like an old woman testing the security of dentures. When it woke, it sucked urgently at her breast, forceful and insistent. She lay awake at night and listened to the baby breathing in the cot beside her, and wondered what she would do if the little chest stopped rising and falling. She realised how little she had thought about the baby during her pregnancy. She had thought only of herself, and of Sam, and now what she felt for the baby could not properly be called love. It was more like fury. And guilt.

Once home, Athena began to read books about child care in a panic. She had left it too late, she reflected, to prepare herself for the emotional shock of the birth — of having this scrap of life emerge from her body. The books told her she would probably feel guilty about leaving Jessica during the day when she returned to work, but instead she felt relief. Jessica's birth, half planned but woefully unprepared for, had shaken her. She had thought it would tie Sam closer to her and knit them into a family, but instead it had left her feeling more vulnerable and less in control than ever before.

For a very short while, it had seemed as though the baby would bring a truce in the tacit battle between them. On the day she had come home from the hospital, he had stood and watched as she changed the baby's nappy.

'What shall we call her?' Athena asked, as she wiped the folds of the little bottom, lifting the doughy legs with one hand.

'What do you think?'

'I don't want any family names,' she said. 'Neither of our families.'

'No. What about Emma?'

She wrinkled her nose and looked at him. He smiled back.

'Rose?'

'They all sound about a century old.'

'Well, she's a wrinkled little bugger.'

He leaned over the changing table and smiled down at the baby. 'Aren't you?' The baby gazed up at him blankly.

He was about to stroke the baby's cheek when the phone rang.

He went to it. 'Hello?' A pause. 'Oh. Hello.'

Athena could tell from his tone that the caller was Dawn.

She lifted the baby over her shoulder and took her out onto the verandah to look at the view over the river. Later, Sam joined them. 'All clean now?' he said. His question was addressed to the baby, but Athena was meant to answer.

'I think I'll call her Jessica,' said Athena. 'My little Jessica.'

'Jessie?' said Sam. 'Jessie is nicer.'

'No. I'm calling my baby Jessica.'

Sam felt the blow. He stood for a while watching her walk up and down, her buttocks like children fighting under a blanket, the baby over her shoulder, her eyes meeting his as she turned towards him, her face hard and unsmiling. Then he left to drive into Newera.

The birth did not change Sam's routine. He punished himself with work, but in spite of his efforts he was falling further and further behind in his mortgage repayments to the bank. He was worn out by the evening, and fell asleep on the floor of the lounge room. But Sam had a sleep problem. In recent months no matter how long and hard he worked he would wake in the small hours of the morning and be unable to slip back into sleep. He lay there in the darkness trying not to think. Sometimes he went to watch Jessica. Sometimes he hauled on his clothes and drove out to Newera, where Dawn would take him day or night into the undemanding warmth of her bed.

It hurt Sam to look at Jessica. On the rare occasions that Athena gave the child to him to hold, he sat frozen by fear at his own tender feelings. The child stared at him with all-knowing eyes, and sometimes Sam would whisper: 'Oh Jessie, Jessie, Jessie. Where have you come from?' He would hug her awkwardly, afraid of crushing her little limbs. He was intoxicated by the warm animal smell of her head, and the reflex grasp of her hand on his fingers. He felt the child drawing him out of his self-containment, but he could not welcome the feeling. He retreated and slipped further from Athena's grasp.

Athena's mother came to stay for a short while, as grandmothers were meant to do, but after a few days of Athena snatching tasks from her hands, both women gave up the pretence and she returned to Adelaide. Athena said to Jean on the phone: 'She was the last person I wanted around.'

'And how's Sam?' Jean asked.

'Still screwing his girlfriend.'

There was a pause. 'If you love something . . .' Jean began. Athena hung up.

Jessica was a placid baby. She rarely cried, and slept through the night within weeks of being brought home. Her eyes were an intense blue that Athena could not relate to either her own or Sam's families. But Jessica was the only thing at peace in the household. Most of the time, the atmosphere — with so much felt and so little said — was enough to make Athena fear she would lose control and run screaming out of the house.

Athena returned to work six weeks after giving birth and found her desk piled high with paper. Uppermost was a copy of the town council minutes. The mayor, Alan Neil, had circled two items in red and written in the margin: 'Athena, see me about these please.'

The first item didn't please her. Councillor Pascoe had been to the Gold Coast for his summer holidays and in Surfers' Paradise had seen a town crier parading the main street, ringing a bell. This, he had found out, was for the entertainment and information of tourists. Full of post-holiday enthusiasm, Councillor Pascoe had successfully moved that the Newera Tourism Officer — Athena — investigate the appointment of an official Newera Town Crier, 'with appropriate costume'.

Athena flicked the page. The second item drawn to her attention was more cryptic. Council had received a report from the Department of Engineering and Water Supply on a new salinity mitigation scheme. The discussion had gone on for some time, and the topics were listed in point form: 'erection of signs', 'visual impact' and 'tackling ill-informed opposition'. Circled in red were the words: 'New lake in Chinky Basin. Tourism possibilities? Action: Ms Masters.'

Athena put the council minutes to one side and opened her mail. The manager of the Big Orange wanted her help to write a promotional leaflet. Several tourism magazines were offering to publish articles on Newera if the council would buy advertising space, and there was a swag of letters from potential visitors wanting tourism information on Newera. Then there was an invitation to a dinner for someone she had never heard of.

She tossed it aside and dealt with the letters first, putting prepackaged collections of leaflets into special Newera envelopes. Athena had ordered these during her first months in the job. She had the power and the budget to do such things. It was one of the things that made this the best job she had ever had — the only one where what she thought mattered. The envelopes were decorated with a picture of an orange with stick limbs, wearing sunglasses and reclining in a deck chair.

Athena put the leaflets in the post, then taking her copy of the minutes in hand, she went and knocked on Alan Neil's door.

At thirty-five, Alan Neil was the youngest mayor Newera had had. He had been sent to Adelaide for his education and had a degree in horticulture. He dressed in a style that marked him out from the other men in the town — check jackets and socks of grey silky material. His hair was neatly parted in front and cut so that the back arranged itself in a perfect spiral from the crown of his head. He had it trimmed every eighth week at the hairdresser's opposite the ferry.

Alan Neil was solid. Looking at him it was impossible to doubt either his competence or his conservatism, but his youth would have counted against him in Newera were it not for the fact that the Neil family, a multi-branched and intermarried collection whose forebears had been on the *Virgin*, were the closest thing the town had to an aristocracy. The Neil family ran Newera. Alan's Uncle Walter was the president of the Rotary Club. His cousin Betty Schenke headed the Country Women's Association, and his brother was the manager of the Newera branch of the State Bank.

Since he was a child, Alan Neil's every action had been seen in terms of who he reminded people of. He would do or say something which he thought precocious and original, only to have legions of aunts and uncles and cousins sigh and say: 'Ah, so like . . .'. Since the comparisons were always made with approval, he had learned to feel as much pleasure in being a perfect manifestation of a Neil as he would have had his merits been seen as his own. To himself and to the outside world, Alan Neil was exactly as he ought to be: a fitting descendant of the pioneers. Had he been told that his ancestors were nothing like him, but had been frightened and confused and sometimes foolish and cruel, he would have felt dispossessed. It would have been as shocking as telling him that he was adopted.

He rose as Athena came in.

'Welcome back. How's the kid? Got a name yet?'

'Jessica,' Athena said. 'We agreed on Jessica.'

'Pretty. And you're well?'

'Perfectly fine.' She was looking haughty.

'Fine, have a seat.'

'The town crier idea . . .' Athena began. She was about to say that it did not appeal to her. She had the words worked out. She was going to say it was 'not appropriate'.

'It's a beauty isn't it? And shouldn't cost a cent except for the costume.'

Athena shifted in her chair. 'There wouldn't actually have *been* a town crier here, would there? I mean in the early days?'

Alan looked puzzled. 'No.'

'Well, wouldn't it be better to have something more to do with the town's history?'

He frowned. 'Like what?'

Athena hesitated. In the few months she had given the job before taking maternity leave, she had realised that what she considered the town's natural attractions — the river, the cliffs and the bird life — were commonplace and dull to those who had been brought up with them. Always they felt the urge to add to them. 'There's nothing to do here,' the locals would say, not realising that people came to do nothing.

'Well, what about doing something with the local Aborigines? There are some around, aren't there? I see them shopping sometimes. Crafts or something.'

Alan picked up his pen and began pushing it against the desk. There was a silence.

'Have you seen where they live? The old mission?'

'No.'

His fingers travelled from the top to the bottom of the pen. He lifted it, turned it over in his fingers, and pushed it against the desk again.

'The town crier would be fun,' he said. 'Something different. We'd get him a bell and a proper uniform.' Alan dropped the pen and his hand circled vaguely around his head. 'You know, one of those hats and,' he fluttered his hand at his neck, 'lace and so on.'

Athena could see she wasn't going to win. 'So who do we get? A volunteer presumably?'

'Advertise. There are a lot of blokes who like clowning around. Someone will take it on.'

She nodded and made a note on her pad. 'And the other thing. Chinky Basin? Where's that?'

'That's a bigger thing.' Alan Neil picked up his pen again and walked over to the map of the district that hung on his wall. He stabbed at an unmarked area to the south of the highway. 'It's here. Nothing-country. Wheat'll barely grow. I'd never heard of it before, but it's where the government's going to put this lake.'

'Lake?'

'You've heard about the salinity scheme?'

'Vaguely.'

'Well, that's where they're going to pump all the water. They reckon it'll cover seven square kilometres. We've got to be able to do something with a water body like that.'

'I don't understand. How's this lake going to get there?'

He scratched the back of his neck with the pen. 'It's technical,' he said. 'Talk to the E&WS about it. They're hot to trot on it. Just brought up a new official to oversee the whole thing. Bruce Pierce — he's in the office next to yours. A very impressive scheme, apparently, though they don't crow about it much.'

'And when will this lake be, um, when will it happen?'

'They start pumping at the end of the year, which means the lake will be full by next autumn. You should talk to Bruce. Find out about it. Put a few things to the council. It should have a lot of potential. Windsurfing, perhaps.'

Athena nodded and rose. It was time to feed Jessica. Her breasts were hurting.

'I'll leave you to it,' she said.

'Right. You're coming to the dinner next week?'

'Dinner?'

'For Tom Linke. Should be an invitation on your desk. He's retiring from running the packing sheds. Everyone's going to be there. You'd better come. You'll get the chance to meet some people.'

'I'll come,' she said, and swept out of the door, feeling her breasts beginning to leak.

*

Athena had advertised for a child minder soon after Jessica was born. It was the end of summer, and the fruit packing shed had been laying off most of the women who worked there during the stone-fruit season, so Athena had been swamped with applications. She chose Barbara McLachlan, wife of the ferryman, who subsidised her husband's drinking and spending habits with casual jobs.

Barbara had the advantage of living only a stone's throw from the council buildings, meaning Athena could walk across to breastfeed the baby several times a day.

Barbara cleaned houses, and baby-sat. She had the contract to clean the local football clubrooms, and in the height of summer she spent days standing in hot corrugated iron sheds cutting apricots in half and laying them on trays for drying. The pay was only two dollars a tray, but Barbara had been doing it since she was a little girl and on a good day she could earn a hundred dollars. The fruit affected her, though. After a day of cutting apricots, Barbara would find herself looking at Bernie, and trying to decide which variety of apricot his alcohol-flushed face most resembled. She hadn't eaten an apricot for years.

Barbara and Bernie live in one of Newera's oldest streets. The houses, set back from the road and screened by pepper trees, had originally been built of corrugated iron, but many of them had been covered with weatherboard or brick veneer or, most recently, plastic cladding textured and moulded to look like brick. As a result, the street had a piebald look and Barbara's house, with its original outer walls of red-painted iron, receded darkly between the pale brick imitations. The living room was in darkness, heavy curtains drawn against the heat. Barbara's own children were in their final years of school, and were rarely at home these days. During the day the house was quiet. Athena sat in a deep armchair and cradled Jessica while Barbara perched on the edge of the opposite chair. Her feet were thrust into heavy sandals she had bought from the chemist. They had raised plastic bumps designed to massage her feet while she walked. One thin arm was resting on her knee, and her hand held a cigarette. She had a black eye.

'How did you get that?' Athena asked, nodding at the bruise.

'Stupid,' Barbara said. 'I walked into the shower rose.' She leaned back, unfolding her thin brown legs. 'Ouch,' she said, and laughed a little.

'You look tired,' said Athena. She was thinking that Barbara was lying.

'I haven't slept.'

The two women's eyes met. Barbara, Athena was dismayed to see, was on the point of tears. She felt an involuntary rush of sympathy. Should she stay and listen, or get out? Jessica had fallen asleep with Athena's nipple still in her mouth. It would be very easy to stay, to chat, to offer sympathy and feel Barbara's admiration and gratitude in return. She resisted the impulse. She had enough to worry about. She couldn't take this on too.

She stood, buttoned her blouse and handed the comatose Jessica to Barbara.

'I'd rather you didn't smoke near the baby,' she said, haughtily. Barbara lowered her entreating eyes.

VI

When Athena first glanced down at the map as it unrolled she almost cried out in panic at what she saw. The thought flashed across her mind: 'It's the farm. It's us. It's us.'

Bruce Pierce, the engineer who had taken over the office next to hers, was leaning over the map, his silk tie swinging from his throat like a limp pendulum as he pointed here and there. The map showed the whole of the southern portion of the continent, but the normal pastels of green and brown were overlaid with thrusting arrows of different widths, all tending towards the stretch of cliffs upstream from Newera, and changing in color from deep blue to urgent red as they neared the river. The arrows showed the flow of underground water, Bruce Pierce said, and the change in color indicated the increasing saltiness of the water as it moved towards the river.

'Its been going on for millions of years,' he said, 'Draining into the river here.' He stabbed at the stretch of cliffs near the farm, then looked up, 'but now it's got to stop.'

CHAPTER THREE

PLUMBING AND THE PEOPLE IN THE SKY

I

For the Ngawait, the sky was not a lonely place, not separate, not remote. It enfolded the terrestrial world and was similar to it. The sun, moon and stars had all once moved on the earth. Sorcerers could visit the sky to gain knowledge, and everyone travelled there after death. The stars were the ancestors. They lived by the white river that wound its way across the night sky, a reassuring echo of the river that ran beneath.

Nurelli came from the sky to create the earth, and returned there when his job was done. From his position in the heavens, he saw a snake crossing the plain. He came down and chased it away, and its windings made the course of the river.

But another story said that an old blind woman called Noorella took two children to guide her on a journey to the sea. The children led her this way and that, sometimes losing their track and doubling back, sometimes running off to play and leaving Noorella to wander alone. Together they made the river, and the billabongs marked the spots where they had camped.

Later, Ngurunderi came down from the sky to chase Ponde, a giant Murray cod. The chase began where the last big river joined the Murray, which was then just a narrow stream. Every time Ngurunderi launched his spear Ponde would sweep his tail and change course, so creating the great bays and reaches of the river. After many days, Ponde reached the big lake at the end of the river and sank beneath the waves, but Ngurunderi did not give up. He waited at the mouth of the lake for Ponde to pass into the sea and, with one mighty throw, finally speared the giant fish. Then he took his flint knife and cut Ponde into seven pieces. One by one, he threw the pieces back into the water, making the first into a silver bream, the second into a perch, the third into a callop, the fourth into a catfish, the fifth into the tiny sprat and the sixth into a mudfish. As he threw the last piece, Ngurunderi said: 'You remain Ponde'. Thus Ngurunderi created all the fish of the river, but the Murray cod remained the greatest.

Then Ngurunderi washed himself in the sea and threw a line back to the sky, where he can still be seen, his star cluster a comfort to the people of the river.

II

The landscape was to be plumbed, Bruce Pierce said. Already, along the sides of the river, rigs were drilling into the limestone and bringing up gouts of water and the dust that settled in puddles: a white, soapy mix. Fifty bores, strung like two daisy-chains on either side of the river, were to be sunk, reaching down hundreds of metres to the slow salty flows below the cliffs.

When the pumps were switched on, each bore would act like a

plughole, capturing the groundwater in slow vortices, creating a series of interconnecting funnels that would drain the landscape like a bathtub. The salt water would be pumped to the surface, then sent surging far away from the river along kilometres of pipe to dry Chinky Basin, where it would spurt out again onto the sand. Each day, fifteen million litres of water, carrying with it a hundred and seventy tonnes of salt, would flow along the pipes and into the lake.

Bruce said the scheme meant fruit growers upstream could continue to protect their orchards from salinity by pumping the rising groundwater out from under their orchards and dumping it in the river. That made the river saltier, of course, but thanks to the Chinky Basin scheme it would all balance out: the Riverland would still have water that wouldn't kill the trees, and Adelaide would still have something to drink.

Bruce said it was the first time in the world that such an ambitious thing had been attempted. 'It's been done in mining,' he said. 'To protect the shafts. Dewatering the landscape. But never before in river management. It really is a feat of engineering. We're quite proud of it, actually.' He fingered his tie and looked up from the map. He was nice, Athena decided, in a sandy, non-descript sort of way. She had recovered from her shock now. She met his eyes and raised one eyebrow at him.

'You must be very excited to be involved.'

'I am.'

It had taken them many months of research to decide on Chinky Basin as the site for the lake, he said. It had to be a natural depression, high up and far enough away from the river not to be at risk of flooding. The salt water would wreck the immediately surrounding country, so it had to be already degraded, and available for purchase by the government. Most important, the soil under the lake had to be dense enough to stop the water from seeping through and finding its way back to the river too quickly.

'But it will flow back eventually?' Athena asked.

'Eventually. In about 50 000 years.'

'And we won't be around.'

'I'd say not.'

'Dust and ashes.'

'I'd say so.'

'The way of all flesh.'

'Er, mmmm.'

Bruce was wondering what was happening. The air in the room seemed strangely charged. In spite or perhaps because of the shock she had got when he first unrolled the map with its accusing arrows, Athena was playing her games. She envied him the ease with which he talked of manipulating things, forcing the landscape to submit. She envied his power. She wanted it.

Bruce began talking again. There was another problem. The engineers called it the hydraulic pulse. The water on Chinky Basin would put pressure on the water already in the landscape. Like turning on a tap at the beginning of a hose pipe, the lake would push other groundwater into the river at a faster pace. Bruce was not worried. 'We've done the tests,' he told Athena. 'We've drilled so many test holes the place looks like a bloody Swiss cheese. We reckon it'll take a hundred years for the pulse to take effect.'

'And then?'

He shrugged. 'We'll take the lake out of service. We'll have thought of something else.'

'It's good,' she said, 'to know this sort of thing can be controlled. Such a big problem.'

He nodded. 'We stop this process,' he jerked a finger at the map. 'Stop a natural process, and we can continue irrigating. An unnatural one.'

'Who would have thought it. It seems so simple. Such control.'

She was genuinely thrilled at the idea. Pumps, pipes and control. She wanted to be part of it.

'Will you take me there?' asked Athena. 'I'm meant to be looking at it, to see what tourism possibilities it holds.'

'Sure,' he said, 'Give us a hoy when you want to go.' As he rolled up his map, he told her it was largely thanks to the Department of Engineering and Water Supply that the name 'Chinky Basin' had been rediscovered. During the week it was nothingland, occupied only by rabbits. On weekends it was taken over by the beaten-up cars and drivers of the Newera Speedway Club, for whom the remoteness and dusty degradation were advantages. Nobody had known that the place had a name, and when Bruce Pierce discovered 'Chinky Basin' written on ancient survey maps, nobody could offer a hint of its origins, so quickly were such things forgotten, and meaning lost.

III

During his brief period of fascination with the ways of the Ngawait, Kingsford Laws once remarked to Thomas Pelican Short that it was easy to see where Aborigines had got the idea for the woomera, since the pelican's beak was exactly the same shape. In his diary, Laws recorded his version of Short's reply.

'Oh no boss. That one smart pelican-man. He once a blackfella, but he keep his woomera wid 'im when he change!'

'Truly,' Laws commented, 'the mythology of the Aborigine is hard to follow, for they have in their language tones for which we can find no expression, and shades of thought we cannot interpret.'

The Ngawait language, which Laws never learned, embraced usefulness. There was a word for rain, a different word for cold-weather rain, and another for the smell of the rain that came after the heat. Plants were understood in terms of their usefulness. Of the two hundred and thirty-three plants that grew in Ngawait territory, all but twenty-nine were of use to somebody: either to humans, or to animals. They could be useful as feed, or as fire-wood, or for shade, or medicine, or to make twine. The remainder were of no use, yet it was said that even these rubbish plants were of use to themselves, since they produced seed and propagated the species.

Europeans came to the river thinking themselves in wilderness, but the country was not wilderness to the Ngawait. The universe and all its parts — plants, animals, weather and sky — were conscious, moral agents. The relationships between them were intended and useful. The world was like a garden, and all the things in it kept to their role and tended to its health.

Wilderness came to the Ngawait. Disease and rabbits came first, before Sturt. The native grasses disappeared. After Sturt, fences went up, new animals were introduced. Some died out. Others over-ran the garden, killing what was there before. Trees were felled and even the river was made to run to a different order.

The Europeans created their garden in the desert, but for the Ngawait, chaos had entered, and turned the garden all to waste.

Only the sky remained the same. That other river ran freely.

The Europeans, feet in civilisation, looked up and felt lonely and small. The river people (while hope lasted) looked up and saw a place where wilderness had not penetrated.

It was the last garden, and in it there was room for an infinite number of stars.

IV

'The Big Orange,' Athena wrote, 'is not only a fun-packed family outing.'

Not even, she thought to herself. She glanced at the picture of the Big Orange that was to go on the cover of the promotional leaflet. Taken so that the fire-escape was hidden from view behind the curve of pock-marked fibreglass, the shot showed grinning children holding glasses of orange juice and hanging out of the third-floor viewing gallery. The sky was blue and studded with cumulus clouds. A smiling family was walking up the ramp to the ground-floor tourist shop, to be greeted by a man in a Bazza the Bunyip suit. Bazza the Bunyip, a reptilian creature with green skin and red tongue, had been created to encourage children not to drop litter on the riverbank.

Athena sighed and took up her pen again.

'It is also an important tribute to the citrus industry, which is the main livelihood of the Riverland region.'

She paused for thought, then pushed on.

'Towering above the attractive green orchards of Newera, the Big Orange is the biggest citrus fruit in the world.'

Were there any big oranges in Florida, or California, she wondered. Quite possibly. She crossed out 'the world' and wrote instead 'the southern hemisphere'. And could an orange be said to tower over orchards? She furrowed her brow. Bulging? Hardly. She crossed out 'towering over' and wrote instead 'Dwarfing the attractive green orchards of Newera . . .'

She counted the number of words. One hundred and fifty more to go. What more could be said?

'The Big Orange incorporates a viewing gallery, a tourist shop where you can purchase attractive mementoes of your visit, and a gallery displaying local artists' perspectives of the citrus industry and the Riverland.'

Athena did another word count, and added 'stunning beauty of' before the word 'Riverland'.

'Built in 1984, the Big Orange is 12 metres high and 37 metres in circumference. It is modelled on a Valencia orange, best known for its excellent juicing properties.'

'Built' was hardly the right word, Athena thought. Grown?

Erected? Put in place? She crossed out the whole phrase and wrote instead:

The Big Orange has graced the Newera orchards since 1984 . . .

It is at one and the same time a tourist attraction, a record-breaking piece of fruit, and a powerful symbol.

Don't forget to make a trip to the Big Orange part of your fun-packed, sun-packed visit to the Riverland. Admission $2. Bazza the Bunyip in attendance on weekends and school holidays only.

Athena put down her pen. After that, she thought, I need a really strong cup of coffee.

V

Semi-trailers made different sounds, Rosie thought, her hand twitching by her side as the pastor's words surfaced above the roar.

I praise the Lord because he guides me.

Normally-laden trucks bellowed along, but you could hear over the noise, except when they were accelerating or braking. By the time they passed the church, Rosie reflected, they were cruising at top speed, and the noise was bearable.

Even at night I feel his leading.

The empty trucks made a more high-pitched sound, no louder, but more invasive. Voices had to be raised. Entire hymns could be sung into the noise, and lost.

I am always aware of the Lord's presence. He is near and nothing can shake me.

It was the wide and high loads that caused the real problems — the mobile homes being shifted up the river, or the big galvanised steel tanks, or the really big loads of hay. You could almost feel such trucks approach, the noise borne on the air they pushed in front of them.

So I rejoice and I am glad.

It was a sound like gravel in a cement mixer, a rushing sound of many tiny disturbances. All other noise was pushed aside.

Even my body has hope, because you will not abandon me in the grave.

When trucks like that went past, you couldn't hear what the pastor was saying, and even the congregation's responses seemed drowned, puny, pushed against the whitewashed walls.

You will not let your faithful one decay.

The sound of the trucks travelled a long way, Rosie thought, especially at night, when no matter how far from the highway you were, you could hear their grunts and roars, like angry animals dashing to and fro. Did the truck drivers read the notice outside the church as they hurtled by?

'You show me the path of life,' the pastor said.

The congregation responded. 'Your presence fills me with joy and brings me pleasure for ever.'

Rosie thought of the truck drivers: big men with their soft bellies slung in singlets, seated in the heads of the roaring beasts. Their own heads would be hollow with lack of sleep, poor things. Their minds would be full of noise. What did they think about the notice Rosie and her friends spent so much time on. Did they think about the message? They were rough men. Did they . . . did they laugh?

Rosie's hand fluttered by her side again as she realised how far her attention had strayed. She struggled to bring her thoughts back inside the church. The congregation was rustling back onto the pews. There were too many flies in the church, Rosie thought. It was distracting. Too many trucks going by outside and too much dust. Sitting, she flicked at her blue woollen skirt.

The church was almost full. Young Dean Nitschke played the electronic organ so nicely, considering his age. Old Mr Schenke sat in his dark suit, ancient hearing aid strapped to his chest and aimed at Pastor Jones who was wearing the stole Rosie had helped embroider with wheat sheaves and oranges. It was three weeks to Easter, and there was a slackening in the heat, but still no rain. The wheat paddocks around the church lay fallow, the red dust easily picked up by the winds. It mingled with the new white dust from the drilling of bores along the clifftop, and the pink mixture came through the sash windows of the church and landed on the pews, the altar, and the Easter eggs the children had used to decorate the church. Easter eggs already in the shops, Rosie thought vaguely. Pagan, her mother would have said. Spring rites. Chocolate. Yet there was no renewal, no spring, here. No rain. It was a time of waiting: after harvest, before sowing.

The pastor called all the children to the front of the church. He held up three plates: paper, plastic and china.

'How long will the paper plate last, if you use it for a barbecue this afternoon?' he asked. A hand went up. It belonged to a young boy Rosie didn't recognise.

'You'd throw it away. It'd be wrecked,' the boy said.

'And this one? How long would the china plate last?'

The same boy's hand went up.

Rosie turned round, looking for the parents of the child.

There she was, the newcomer, sitting in the back corner next to the electronic organ — a seat regular members of the congregation knew better than to use. Her hair was streaked blonde, her skin was sallow. She wore a white drop-waisted dress that fell from her shoulders, revealing nothing of her body, and on her face was a look of foreboding mixed with pride.

'That's right. We hope it will last for a long time, but we might drop it when we're drying up tonight and break it. We really can't know. What about the plastic one?'

The boy's hand was up again. 'It'd last for a hell of a long time,' he said.

Pastor Jones laughed a little. 'Yes, but eventually it will crack or break.'

He put the plates down and folded his hands in front of him. 'Only one thing lasts forever, boys and girls. Who can tell me what that is?'

There was a silence, then the little boy's hand shot up. He was excited this time, jigging around, his socks falling to his ankles. The pastor nodded at him.

'Saucers, 'cos we never use them. We use mugs,' the boy said.

Rosie's hand flew to her mouth. The congregation tittered. The boy's mother closed her eyes.

'No,' the pastor said sharply, then more softly. 'No. You know that God's love lasts forever. No matter where you are, or what you do, God loves you. Now go back to your seats, and enjoy the singing.'

Rosie saw the boy run to his mother, clamber onto her lap and whisper into her ear. She caressed his hair, and smiled.

After the service, tea was served from trestle-tables put up in the shade cast by the sign. Rosie carried the newcomer a cup, clasping it close to her to protect it from the dust and cooling wind.

'I hope you take sugar.'

'Oh. Ta.'

The pastor introduced them. 'Dawn Bingham, meet Rosie Thomas. Rosie is one of the pillars of our little congregation.' He clutched both women briefly on the upper arms, as though to commend them to each other, and moved away.

'You're new . . . aren't you? In the area . . . in Newera?'

'We've been here since just before Christmas,' Dawn said. 'But we haven't met many people yet.'

'Well it's very nice to see you here.'

'I want Matthew to know about God,' Dawn said, a little defensively. 'He can chuck it out later if he wants, but I want him to have it to fall back on.'

As though, Rosie thought, the knowledge could do her no good at all.

Reading her thoughts, Dawn added: 'I went to church once. Every week.'

'Oh . . . yes.'

In fact, Dawn had once been a very religious, neat girl — always helpful and clean. Her mother told her she was a treasure. She walked around with her lips pursed, gently smiling, aware of her own goodness. Then she turned seventeen and in the summer of that year, like a flash of lightning, came the illness of love, and she found herself in the back of a panel van at the drive-in with her white dress around her neck. She got pregnant. Her love affair fell apart. Her family deserted her. She was suddenly shut off from her neat, good self. She didn't know who she was, if she was not the angel she had fancied herself to be.

Now she played the scrubber. She picked up men because she thought it was what her sort of person did. Also, of course, she was lonely. On the surface, she was hard-bitten and hungry, like a sharp little bird after worms, yet a part of her was still shocked at how easy, good and inconsequential sex could be.

In Newera, away from the people who knew of her fall, she had thought she might be able to be someone else. When she was first enfolded by the false warmth of Athena, she had thought she might be 'a treasure' to someone again. Vacuuming that floor, she had been happy. That had gone wrong. She was trapped in her hard, brittle, bird-like self. But Matthew must be safeguarded. Doors to consolation must never be closed to him. In Newera, she had decided, they would be church-goers.

'Well, he learnt something today didn't he,' Rosie said, smiling down at the child.

'Hopeless,' Dawn said. 'He's had no religion 'till we came here. They made nativity scenes at infants' school last Christmas. He brought it home, and I had to ask who this little fat man was that he'd made out of Playdo. You know what he said?'

The Adelaide to Sydney bus was approaching, threatening to drown out conversation. Rosie shook her head.

'Round John Virgin!' Dawn shouted. 'He said it was Round John Virgin.'

'John?' Rosie murmured, her voice swallowed by the approaching bus. Apostle John? she wondered. Little John?

'That's right! Round John Virgin. You know, "round yon virgin mother and child". The little bugger.' Dawn took her son's hand and smiled down at him as the bus roared past.

The notice board shook in the slipstream, squeaking and clanging as though likely to fall over. The motto for the week was: ETERNAL LIFE. BE IN IT.

'Oh I see,' said Rosie, who didn't. 'Let me get you another cup, that one's full of dust.' And she approached the urn, cup in hand, murmuring to herself. 'Round John. Round John.' It was nonsense, she thought, and felt the familiar vague frustration and alarm at how easily meaning could elude her reverent, musing mind.

CHAPTER FOUR

THE TOWN CRIER

I

In Newera, social status was conferred largely on the basis of the number of floods you could remember, since it was these watery dislocations, the turmoil they caused and the type and extent of rebuilding which followed that marked the phases of town history in the collective consciousness. The big flood had been in 1957, a year the rest of the world thought of as the beginning of the space age. But for a generation along the banks of the Murray, the new pumping station, the man on the moon, the Cuban missile crisis and the Pill had all come 'after the flood', and the pioneering years, two world wars and several depressions were 'before'.

It was the Neil boys who had turned out in the middle of the night to sandbag the pumping station, but the river got in nevertheless. Meanwhile, Emma Neil, left all alone, had gone into labour and rowed herself across the torrent in the moonlight to give birth to a son in the warm mud by the side of what used to be the football field, but had become the river. It was said there had never been a flood in Newera without the Neils.

The first Alan Neil was an Adelaide bricklayer, who had come home from looking for work to find his furniture taken by the bailiff and his wife and their three children sitting in the dust. Three weeks later they were on their way to Newera, aboard the *Virgin* as it churned upstream, the gums slipping past darkly and the engine drowning the splashing and calling of the night.

The oldest son was named after his father. At sixteen, he lied about his age, spent three months training, travelled half a world away from the hard South Australian light and was gunned down within a week of arriving in France. His name appeared in tarnished gold lettering on the Newera roll of honour in the Institute hall, the first of the handful who did not return from foreign wars.

The name Alan skipped a generation, then young Ken Neil married, and pleased his parents by naming his first-born after his dead hero uncle. The present-day Alan Neil was that man's son, and his grandfather Ken, long since retired from running the family fruit block, was now the oldest surviving member of the family.

Athena met him on the night of Tom Linke's retirement dinner, which, like most social events, was held at the pub. Everyone connected with Linke and his career had been invited: his family, which, through marriage, included most of the other families in town; his friends, who, since bad feeling could not be admitted in such a small community, included his enemies; and his employees — the foremen and the workers who packed the fruit.

Athena spent considerable time deciding what to wear. The invitation said 'lounge suit', which gave her no hint, other than that jeans or a cotton smock would not do. It was, in any case, a long time since Athena had been able to fit into her jeans. She finally hit on a white satin kaftan she had sewn herself, in which she knew she looked uncompromisingly large, aloof and queenly. These were qualities she felt she would need to negotiate successfully an event at which she would be the only stranger.

She had hoped Sam would come, but he didn't own a suit, which gave him the perfect excuse, without the need for emotional confrontation. Or so he thought.

'You could hire one, or buy one,' she had said.

'No.'

'We never meet people together.'

'No. We don't.'

'It upsets me.'

Silence.

'You'll stay at home then, and look after Jessica. Your daughter. You won't . . . .'

'I'll stay. I'll stay.'

Athena had to park almost halfway up the hill, the street was so crowded. As she walked down towards the lights of the pub, she felt not so much a chill as a slackening in the heat: the first signal that the monotonous warmth of summer was giving way to autumn. The night sky, limpid for many weeks, was blurred with the faintest suggestion of mist.

A group of town toughs in torn jeans and dirty singlets were sitting on the steps of the pub as Athena swept towards the double doors. They looked up, aware of her bulk and that she was alone.

'Hey, Big Bertha. Give us a kiss,' slurred one of them, puckering his lips.

Athena smiled at him in her best queenly manner and swept on, but the crushing effect she had hoped for was spoilt when she tripped on the doormat and half fell through the doors and into the middle of pre-dinner drinks. She hurtled in, struggling to keep on her feet and was aware of a roomful of bellies, brown suits and lace blouses, all turned towards her in alarm, while behind her the boys choked with laughter.

'Upsadaisy,' a man's voice said, and a hand gripped her elbow.

Regaining her balance, she looked up and saw a face that looked vaguely familiar. It was peach-like: round, ruddy, weathered soft and creased in the right places for its fullness to be accommodated.

'Ken Neil,' the man said, offering her his hand with a shy, downward glance. Taking it, Athena realised it was not his face she had seen before, but his family's.

He was an old man. His chest was hollow and his hair, which he had combed with water and plastered across his scalp, was white, yet his grip on her arm had been firm enough to stop her from falling.

'Athena Masters. I work with your grandson,' she said. 'He's my boss.'

'Athena, my dear. My dear! Did you hurt yourself?' Rosie Thomas, buttoned into a navy blue suit with a Peter Pan collar, had joined them. She patted Athena's satin clad arm.

'Athena. How nice. You've met Ken . . . met my brother?'

'Not until now,' said Athena. 'I didn't realise you were a Neil too, Rosie.'

Rosie and Ken smiled simultaneously, the resemblance between them suddenly apparent. Ken and his grandson the mayor had the same chin disappearing into neck, the same hairline and the same folds in the face, but Ken and Rosie shared subtler things: a diffidence and unwillingness to presume, which sat oddly with their family pride.

'We get around,' said Ken. 'We Neils.'

Rosie was concerned. 'Athena, would you like . . . I mean, not if you'd rather not . . . but if you don't know anyone, would you like to join us? On our table? She must, mustn't she Ken?'

'Ah yes. Most welcome. Just the family and a few friends. Most welcome.'

Athena's undignified entrance had unsettled her, destroying the aloofness she had depended on to see her through the evening. In front of her, above the blouses and the brown suits, were familiar faces seen in the street but to which she could not attach names, and inside she felt the loneliness, the sour, anxious breath, of not having Sam with her.

'That,' she said, 'would be very sweet of you.'

The Neil family and their friends had been placed only one step back from the head table, at which sat Tom Linke and Alan Neil and their wives. Ken sat down awkwardly, his legs protruding from under the tablecloth and moving restlessly, as though they were not used to being still. His trousers had ridden up to expose a portion of skin, soft and white, veined in mauve, above his woollen sock. They were, Athena thought, the sort of socks that would normally be worn with work boots, rather than with the shiny polished lace-ups he had on this evening. It occurred to her that, for all his social position, the old man was as uncomfortable as she was and she felt a rush of tenderness for him.

Rosie had moved away to talk to the other women in the clan, and Ken was obviously struggling to find something to talk about.

'Do you like gardening?' he said at last.

'Not really.' Then, seeing his face fall, she added: 'But I'd like to learn.'

'Good time to plant tomatoes now,' he said. 'It's not too cold yet. Plant 'em now and they'll see you through to the first frost.'

Athena nodded.

'Plenty of compost, or manure if it's well rotted.'

Athena nodded again. His legs kicked uneasily underneath the table. He didn't seem to have anything else to say. Uncharacteristically, to make him feel more comfortable, she took up the burden of the conversation.

'Have you known Tom Linke for long?' she said. He nodded and pointed at the top table. 'His wife there. She's a Neil too. My cousin.' His fingers drummed on the tablecloth.

'You must go back a long way?'

'In the flood he and my dad and me spent days up to our thighs in water, untying the sultana grapes from the trellises.'

'Why did you do that?'

'Stupid idea. We hoped they'd float and survive. Didn't work of course. It was his idea. We were desperate. The orange and lemon trees had gone under. We had orchards on the higher ground too, but they died in the drought. No pumping station, no water, and everything else flooded.'

'Tough times,' Athena said.

He was warming up now. 'Another flood,' he said, still gazing at the tablecloth rather than at Athena. 'My brother's appendix went bung. Rowed him out into the dark. No lights. Didn't know whether we were in the right spot or not.'

'But you got him there okay?'

'Yes. That's him over there. Walter. The baby.' Athena turned her head and saw the younger Neil brother, pouring white wine into his glass. His face was flushed, his tie was threatening to land in the wine. He looked none the worse for his watery ordeal.

'Yes, the river's a treacherous beast,' Ken Neil said. 'Never trust the river, is what we used to say.' He paused and for the first time raised his milk-and-water eyes to meet Athena's. 'I'm eighty, you know. Eighty years old,' he said. 'And I'm not a bad cook.'

Now it was Athena who was unsure what to say, but Rosie was returning bearing glasses of sweet sherry. She laid a hand fondly on Ken's shoulder.

'I've been telling Miss Masters about untying the grapes,' he said.

'Oh. Oh yes. The Neils and Linkes go back a long way,' said Rosie. 'Grandma wrote a poem for old Mrs Linke. They knew each other right from the first.' She looked at the ceiling, eyes narrowed, trying to remember the words.

Alan Neil was doing the rounds of the room, trying to persuade people to sit down. As the crowd began to drift towards the tables and divide, the hierarchy of seating arrangements became clear.

Behind the Neils' table were the middle management of the packing sheds and their families. At the back were the people who worked packing the fruit. Athena caught site of Barbara and Bernie. She waved, and Barbara half turned towards her before Bernie, best shirt strained over his belly, caught her by the elbow and guided her towards the back of the room. Barbara, Athena realised with some alarm, was already tipsy. While she watched, Barbara drained her sherry and waved the glass under Bernie's nose in a request for more. Then Athena lost sight of them. Rosie was breathing in her ear.

'This is it. This is what grandma wrote for old Mrs Linke.' She began to recite. 'In 1893 we joined the band of worthy souls who took this land, with fire and work and water clear to make a pleasant garden here . . . oh dear, how does it go.'

The soup plates were being thumped down on the tables. There were two kinds — mixed vegetable and pumpkin. Each variety was served to alternate people, and it was up to the diners to negotiate swaps.

Alan Neil was on his feet striking a glass with his soup spoon but Rosie had remembered some more of the poem.

'Ah yes. This is it. The butter and the bacon too in deadly heat bade us adieu, the ants delighted saw us come and welcomed us to our new home . . . oh dear I've lost it again. Such a lovely poem.'

The room fell silent, but for Barbara's slurred voice, clear in the sudden quiet: 'I want pumpkin, Bernie. Give it to me, you mean bugger.'

'Ladies and gentlemen,' Alan Neil said. 'I ask you to rise for the loyal toast.'

Athena had already lifted her soup spoon, but dropped it hurriedly and stood. Ken filled her glass with wine.

'To Queen Elizabeth in this the thirty-seventh year of her reign, and to all her descendants,' Alan Neil said. They drank, and Athena was about to sit down again when Alan called on his grandfather to say grace. Chins folded over the fat knots of ties. Athena kept her eyes open and saw that nobody else did, except for Ken, who was talking to God in a conversational tone which suggested that He was either at his elbow, or non-existent and therefore able to be treated casually.

'Dear Lord, thank you for your many gifts: our way of life in this peaceful community, sunshine, good friends, our families and children. Thank you also for Tom, who has enriched our lives, and thank you for the food you have laid before us tonight.'

They sat down, and the murmur of conversation began to rise again. The soup was cold.

Rosie leaned towards Athena, breathing lavender scents, and whispered: 'This is the bit about old Mrs Linke. Our neighbours came to settle down in scrub and wild. There walked into my home one day, into my heart, and there to stay, a lady true with eyes of brown, with upright form, voice sweet in tone . . . oh dear.' Rosie pulled herself upright again, then clutched Athena's arm. 'This is it. I've got it now. The bullocks came the scrub to clear, our door they passed on track so near. Oh dear I've lost it again. I am silly. Do you remember it, Ken? Grandma used to tell it to us.'

Ken shook his head, and reached over to fill Athena's glass. She was surprised to see that she had emptied it so quickly. It was the first wine she had drunk since her pregnancy, and she could feel it going to her head.

The main courses were being served: beef or chicken, each with identical thick gravy and distributed in the same fashion as the soups. Athena could hear Barbara braying at the waitress, and wondered if she drank while minding Jessica.

Alan Neil was on his feet again. He was, Athena thought, the only person in the room who didn't look out of place in a suit. Rosie and Ken sat nodding their heads with pleasure, but Alan's words came to Athena in snatches. She was straining to hear what was going on at Barbara's table, where there seemed to be some disturbance.

'Always showed courage through hardship . . . transformed the way we market, produce and pack oranges . . .' Alan Neil said.

'And bloody hard work it was too,' came Barbara's voice.

'Shut up, you bitch,' hissed Bernie.

'Don't you tell me what to do.'

'Just be quiet, why don't you.'

'You can't tell me what to do.'

'Yeah. Yeah. Just shut up.'

'But Tom will best be remembered for pioneering the new irrigation areas opened in the 1960s. Five hundred and fifty acres of grazing land were converted to orchard. Five thousand four hundred sprinklers were set in place, and Green Heights grew up to add to the prosperity of our region.'

'Yes, yes, all that bloody water,' Barbara said. 'All those trees.' She waved her hand over her head in an imitation of an overhead sprinkler. 'Woosh. Woosh,' she said. The other faces in the room remained stubbornly fixed on Alan Neil.

'Where before there was only dirt, thanks to Tom Linke, we now have the deep greens of prosperity.'

Alan sat down to applause and Bernie was pushing Barbara unsteadily towards the door.

The main course was cleared away and slabs of cake and sweet dessert wine appeared. Athena was having trouble focusing. Her field of attention had narrowed to the people immediately around her.

'It'll never work,' Walter said. 'What's to stop it all just running back into the river?'

'But they've done research on that . . .' said Ken.

'If you ask me, what they need is a pipeline to the sea. It's the only way you'll ever get rid of all that salt.'

'Or make the river your drain. Put the salt water in that, and bring the fresh in a pipe.'

'You'll never get that up. The trees'd die. The greenies . . .'

'They're dying now. Can't you see it? Thinning out. They're dying now.'

Rosie leant towards Athena with an explanation. 'It's all about this big salt lake. Pumping all that water . . . a big silver lake . . .' she waved an arm vaguely towards the east. 'Out there, where no one will see it.'

'I know,' said Athena, trying not to slur her words. 'I'm meant to be looking into tourism possibilities.'

'Oh. Lovely. They're drilling the bores, you know, along the cliffs near the church.'

'Mmm.'

'So much dirt. The dust!'

Athena was thinking that she should find some coffee, sober up and get home. Through the alcoholic haze, she could feel her breasts hurting. It was time for Jessica's feed.

Then, suddenly, someone was looming over her. Looking up, she saw that a man and woman had come into the room from the bar next door. They were Aborigines, and the man was drunk. His shirt hung open and his fly was half undone, his jeans stained with grog and what looked like vomit. The woman was trying to drag him back into the bar, but he was too drunk to respond. He keened towards the laden tables, listing over Athena.

Walter was on his feet, hands outstretched but not quite touching the couple, as though they were hens he had to encourage back into a coop.

'Out now,' he whispered furiously. 'This is invited guests only. Out now please. You can drink at the bar if you wish.'

The couple left the room, the woman looking only at the ground, the man's eyes jumping in his head.

Walter returned to the table, shook his head, picked up his napkin, and said to Ken: 'What can you do?' He got no reply. Instead, Ken turned to Athena and said: 'You must come out and see my garden some time, Miss Masters. Dinner? Soon? You and your . . . and your . . . your . . .'

And Rosie said: 'Ah yes. Ah yes.'

The road home was a grey ribbon in the moonlight, and the mallee trees leapt out blackly. When Athena got out of the car at the top of the driveway, she took a few moments to catch her breath and was again aware of the slackening in the heat. Looking up at the sky, she was surprised to see two perfect haloes of misty light around the moon. It was the sort of thing, she thought, that would once have been seen as an omen, for good or ill. She stood there for some time, gazing up at the silver heavens, head swimming and breasts aching, listening to the roar of the semi-trailers on the highway and to the smaller, subtler sounds of the cooling night.

II

Athena sat in Barbara's living room. Jessica was almost asleep at her breast. Barbara was wandering from the living room to the bedroom, limbs all wiry and tense, mouth fixed, her voice rising and falling, full of fragile determination.

'I told him. I've told him a hundred times. If you ever hit me again, I'll leave.'

Athena uttered the conventional wisdom. 'No woman should stay with a man who hits her.'

'It happened a couple of times when we were first married, and

I told him then.' Barbara stood, thin legs apart, one hand on her hip. She raised her finger at Athena. 'If you ever lay another hand on me, I'll be off.'

Athena shifted Jessica's weight on her lap, and the baby's pouting lips slipped off her nipple. The eyelids, traced with blue, were closed but the mouth stayed slightly open, a cupid bow, breathing soft, milky smells.

It was obvious that Barbara was longing to talk. Athena was torn between curiosity, which she knew was apt to turn to sympathy, and a desire not to get involved. Most of all, she was worried about her child minding arrangements.

'So where will you go?'

Barbara was carrying an armful of laundered underwear from the couch. With her free hand she picked up a pair of cotton knickers, scrutinised them, and sniffed suspiciously at the crotch. They passed muster.

'Well, I'm not sure,' she said, and suddenly she was smiling. 'You see, I've got a fella.'

She sat down, the underwear spilling from her lap. Athena saw her bright eyes, the excitement so close to panic, and thought, she's in love.

'You know that song on the radio?' Barbara said. She sang, her hand ascending in the air with the tune. 'It started with a k-i-i-ss.' Her hand dropped to her lap again. 'Well, that's my favourite song now, because that's how it started.'

She leant back, laundry dropping around her. 'Strange thing is,' she said, 'I've known him forever. I had a crush on him when I was sixteen. But he didn't know me.'

Athena glanced at Jessica. Fast asleep. Curiosity won.

Barbara had not been a wild teenager. She had not run away from home, or been in trouble with the police, and her pregnancies had occurred only after her marriage. But there were only two ways to be an acceptable teenage girl in Newera, and Barbara had chosen the more controversial. She had scorned the girls whose exercise books were always neat, whose hair always shone and who chatted only with each other. Barbara had chosen the other path. She was a football groupie.

'I wasn't bad-looking then,' Barbara said. 'All the fellas used to take me out. 'Till Bernie.'

What had turned to wire and grimness in her thirties had then been lusty thinness. It had been natural that she, as most desired girl, should end up with the captain of the footie team. Bernie McLachlan had been a muscular lad, everyone's mate, with the shifty-eyed charisma often possessed by men who cannot bear to be alone. He was always going to be Barbara's future but, just as the neat, shiny-haired girls mooned over pop stars, Barbara had a football hero. Bob Grant, blue-eyed ruckman for Glenelg, hung over her bed in sparkling color, football impossibly balanced on the tips of his fingers, as though suspended by a mystic force. Barbara bought newspapers solely so she could cut out every word written about him. She had sent away for a signed picture. She kept this one by her bed. Once, when Glenelg toured the Riverland at the end of the season, she had joined the crowd and gained another autograph.

That had been during her last year of school, and her last year as a single girl. By the next football season she was heavily pregnant and felt many years older. Bernie had found work on the ferry, and spent the evenings training or drinking with his mates. The following year, he moved to night-shift and gave up training. Football faded from Barbara's life, except as one of many excuses for Bernie's absence.

Barbara had never been idealistic about marriage, but was nevertheless soon disappointed in Bernie. In the early years, she was too preoccupied with children to brood but once they were at school she had too much time alone. Now she was thirty-five, but felt much older. Her children were teenagers and didn't need her. She was miserable, and Bernie's spending habits, a substitute for the excitement of his youth, had grown with his beer belly.

'I told him,' Barbara said, now leaning forward with a cigarette in her hand. 'I told him a thousand times. "One more new car, one more credit card, and it's over. Finito". "What's it to you?" he says, and I say "I can manage, you know. I earn money too. Don't think it's your piddling money that pays all the bills."'

Barbara had lost track of Bob Grant's career, although she knew he no longer played for the team. Then, a month ago, she had seen him again. The Glenelg team had done a promotional tour of the Riverland to open the season. Barbara, who had a regular job cleaning the football club rooms, had been hired for the night to serve drinks and trays of asparagus rolls and oysters on crackers.

'He's still with the club,' Barbara said. 'They gave him a job on the management side. I nearly died. He looked so tall.' He was dressed in grey slacks and a club blazer, buttoned over his belt. His hair was thinner, but his eyes were still blue and his smile was the same as the one he had worn when he looked down at her each night from her bedroom wall.

'Thank you,' he said, as he took one of the flaccid pieces of tinned asparagus, shrouded in white bread. She watched his lips move as he ate it, and saw the wedding ring on his finger.

'You a local girl?' he asked, looking at her out of the corner of his eye as he popped the tip of the asparagus spear into his mouth.

'Yep.' She felt vestiges of the bright girlishness she had had when he had been her hero.

'Lucky Newera,' he said.

Barbara told Athena: 'It was just flirting at first. But it was lovely.' She shivered. 'God, he was nice.'

Bob kept up the flirting, and did a mock waltz with her to music from the juke box, egged on by the members of the team.

'He was so tall. He rested his chin on my head,' she told Athena.

The tension between them reached a point where she was suddenly nervous. She moved away. He followed her to the kitchen and there, without smiling, he touched her arm and said: 'I'm just aching to kiss you.'

They went into the back corridor near the garbage bins, where no one else would come. She raised her lips to his, and felt his tongue enter her mouth and his body press against hers. Her undoing was the regard, the tenderness, with which he touched her. She could not remember having been touched that way before.

'He was so soft,' she said to Athena, and sighed. She sang again: 'It started with a k-i-i-i-ss.'

The club had spent a week touring the Riverland towns. Barbara and Bob arranged to meet most nights, when Bernie was at work. She drove up or down the river to wherever he was. He would open his motel room door and she would sink into his arms.

'You're such fun,' he would say. 'I think my wife has forgotten how to have fun.'

There was fresh white bread and milk in the fridges of the motel rooms, intended for breakfast, but they ate it hungrily after making love. She soon saw how much he had aged. He wore his blazer buttoned in order to hide the pot belly that bulged on both sides of his belt. But when she touched him his whole body jumped and his penis sprang instantly erect. She curled her own wiry body into the hair on his chest, and felt the warmth and the bulk of him. When he climbed on top of her, pumped away and expired in ecstasy, she felt tears coming to her eyes, and she prayed to a God she could not recall believing in. Her prayer was a prayer of thanks.

'I mean, how lucky can you get,' she said to Athena. 'How many people end up with their hero?'

The football tour came to an end. Bob returned to Adelaide. Barbara was grief-stricken and so, she believed, was Bob. She had said to him: 'It's over between me and Bernie. I want to be with you.'

And he, lying on the bed, his chest still heaving, had said: 'I'll tell Heather. It'll be hard. I'll tell her, and you can come down to Adelaide. We'll live together.'

'And did he tell her?' Athena asked.

'Not yet. He's going to. But I can't stand it any longer. I'm off.'

The night before Tom Linke's retirement dinner Bernie had come home more than usually drunk, and had sunk with a fart into the bed beside her. The next morning she confronted him about money. He called her a slut. He hit her in the stomach.

'That was the second time he's hit me this year,' Barbara said.

'The black eye?' Athena asked. 'It wasn't the shower rose?'

'I didn't think you'd bought that one.'

Barbara had comforted herself with a drink, and then another, and then another. She remembered very little of the dinner that night, but afterwards she and Bernie had had a row and she had told him she was leaving.

'He cried,' Barbara said. 'Like a big bloody boy. I had to tell the kids he was sick.'

'So what's going to happen now?' Athena asked.

'Bob. He still needs time,' Barbara said, 'before he leaves her. Then I'll go down to Adelaide and we'll live together.' Her eyes were shining. 'It feels like . . . like heaven. Like I'm just going to float up . . .' her hand fluttered over the pile of underwear. 'I'm going to float up into the stars.' Her hand fell. 'It'll be a little while. But I'm moving out now anyway. I'm moving into the flats.'

The flats were the only rental accommodation available in Newera. A two-storey block surrounded by dust and wrecked cars, they were occupied mostly by itinerant men, and were frequently visited by the police.

'I've told Bob. I said to him: "Okay, I understand you need time, but please don't take too long, 'cos I just can't hack it alone. I really can't hack it alone." I'll still need the money, so I'll still take Jessica,' Barbara said. 'It's no further from your work.' She paused. 'I've told Bernie a thousand times that I'd leave. Well. Now I've got a fella, and I'm off. Off into heaven.'

She rose from the armchair and came to take Jessica from Athena's arms. 'You'll have to be getting back to work,' she said. Athena roused herself, buttoned her blouse and heaved herself out of the armchair. She thought of laying a sympathetic hand on Barbara's shoulder, but it seemed inappropriate. She was already moving briskly from cupboards to suitcase and she showed no need for sympathy. Athena lumbered out.

How could Barbara so recklessly throw herself into a situation over which she had no control? How could she take such risks? And yet Athena envied her lack of hesitation in asking a man to give up his wife and family to be with her. The audacity of it! Athena barely dared ask Sam to make her a cup of tea, so fraught was the power struggle between them. And she was far too nervous about the result to ask him to give up Dawn.

If Bob failed Barbara, she would lose everything. What would remain in life for her? It was too much, Athena thought, just too much, that the cleaning lady from Newera should end her days with her teenage football hero. It wouldn't be fair for Barbara to throw herself open without a thought for safety, and to have her trust vindicated. The world just didn't work like that.

'She is braver than me,' Athena thought, and then: 'She is more stupid than me.'

Part of Athena wanted Barbara's adventure to end badly. Otherwise, what was there to be said for the struggle, the exacting effort of remaining apart, of not giving in to the ferment of feeling — not letting the chaos inside?

III

It was Saturday, and awful. Jessica had been crying all afternoon. By the time dark came, she was screaming. Athena knew the baby needed sleep, but she wouldn't be still, let alone relax enough to nap. Mother and daughter's emotions ricocheted off each other. When Sam came in from the farm, they were both frantic and in tears.

Athena felt helpless, which always made her angry. She thrust Jessica into Sam's arms, although his overalls were covered in grease.

'Take her away. Please. Before I do something to her. Please.'

'What should I do?' he said, feeling the hot weight of the screaming child.

'Just get her away from me.'

He looked down at Jessica's contorted face. The noise was shattering. He carried her into the bedroom.

'What do I do?' he called again to Athena.

'Talk to her. Sing to her. Just shut her up,' Athena screamed. 'Do it!'

He sat on the edge of the bed, Jessica on his knee. Her screams stopped only when she needed to draw breath.

'Hello Jessica,' said Sam.

She choked a little as she drew the next lungful of air.

'Hello Jessica,' he said again.

She screamed, but with less determination, blue eyes watching him.

'Um. There was a butterfly,' he said, surprising himself with his words.

Her screaming subsided a little more.

'A butterfly . . .'

Her little body was still stiff, her fists clenched with tension.

'A butterfly . . .' She was drawing another breath, ready to scream again.

'. . . and a flower,' he said hurriedly. 'A butterfly and a flower. And the butterfly . . . .'

He had her attention now. Her little body was relaxing. He saw the soft curve of her cheek, wet with tears. He rocked her a little, and saw her eyes blink, her eyelashes meeting the down on her cheek.

'And the butterfly,' he said. 'The butterfly kissed the flower.'

He paused. There were no more words in him. He didn't know where those had come from. He ducked his head forward and blinked his eye on her cheek, giving her a soft, butterfly kiss with his eyelashes. Jessica's mouth fell open. She brought her little clenched fist to her cheek and touched the spot he had touched. Their eyes met. Sam felt his face smile.

'. . . kissed the flower . . .' he said, and he brushed her cheek again with his eyelashes, feeling the wet of her tears on his own cheek.

She was smiling back at him now. Then, suddenly, she yawned and closed her eyes.

'. . . the flower . . .'

She was asleep. Sam laid her in her cot, then wrapped his empty arms around himself. Where had all that come from? Some buried part of himself. He had once made up stories like that. It was something . . . something he could not afford to be. He had never been so frightened.

Athena blocked the light from the open doorway.

'What did you do? Knock the brat out?' she said.

'No. No, I didn't.'

'What did you do?'

'I told her a story.' He was still spellbound by the sleeping infant.

'What was it? Must have been good.' Athena sensed something significant in the air. She scented emotion. She wanted it. She approached.

'What did you tell her?' she asked more gently.

He was about to reply when he felt her big, heavy hand on his shoulder, and below it he sensed the flesh on her arm and all the bulk of her. He flinched, feeling the heaviness of her grasp on him. The words 'about a butterfly' evaporated from his mind and, instead, he said: 'Just a story.'

'What story?'

Why could she not let him go? Under her questioning, her probing, the special feeling in him died, and the answers he might have given voluntarily lost their attraction.

'Just a story,' he said again, and he moved away from her hand and into the bright light of the living room, where he sank in front of the television.

IV

Bernie McLachlan had no hips and thin little legs. His trousers rode under his stomach and seemed to be constantly at risk of falling down. He wore t-shirts in summer and windcheaters and flannelette shirts in winter. Usually, unless he had just rearranged himself, a few inches of hairy stomach could be seen protruding above his belt. He was scarcely aware of it, except when one of the barmaids, returning after fetching a tray of glasses, would reach out and tickle him on the overhang of soft white flesh. That was the kind of man Bernie was. Women could do that to him without getting the look of resentment and hunger that such an action would provoke from most of the men. Bernie talked about sex all the time, but he was perfectly safe. Anybody could laugh at Bernie. As football captain he had been town hero. Now he had made an easy transition to town clown. If he resented the change he didn't show it, or at least not in the pub. He was a good mate, Bernie. A joker.

Now he was sitting on a bar stool, looking like a bean bag balanced on a stick. His voluptuous curves hung over the tiny vinyl-covered pedestal and his bony elbows were resting on the bar. Out of habit, he thought that he should have been home hours ago, but the idea did not bring its usual pleasurable feeling of independence and defiance. Barbara was not there, not fuming at his absence. She had left. The silly thing was that now home was the only place Bernie wanted to be, except that it would mean being alone.

In the last week, he had tried many times to persuade Barbara to return, only to have the phone slammed in his ear or the door in his face. He had wept — something he thought he had forgotten how to do. Now he was at a loss, and desperate. He had told Barbara that he loved her, that he was sorry, that he would change. He hoped all this was true, but the fact was her going had provoked in him, not so much grief or jealousy as panic. Without Barbara to rebel against, abuse and ignore, Bernie McLachlan was lost — nobody. It was like death, he thought. And now he was frightened at nights on the ferry. It would be so easy to slip into the grey water. He wept at the thought. Poor Bernie, he thought. So unloved.

His mates in the pub knew of her desertion. Who didn't know? You couldn't keep a thing like that quiet in Newera. Of course, none of the blokes embarrassed him or themselves by admitting that he might be seriously upset. Nevertheless, they tried to cheer him, jollying him along. And now Bernie was grinning, as he felt obliged to do, to show he was okay. It had just been suggested to him that he should put in for the job of town crier.

Had Bernie's mates spoken to Athena, they could have saved the council the cost of an advertisement. Bernie was the only man in town likely to dress up in frills, frock coat and funny hat, and willingly draw attention to himself.

'You'd be good, Bernie,' said Ben.

'Yeah,' said Bernie, playing up to it. 'Yeah. I reckon.'

'Seriously. You should go and see about it.'

'So who do I see?'

'That fat bird up at the tourism place. Ath . . . Athey something. Hah. We'll get you a bell and all, Bernie. You'll be beaut, mate.'

Athena Masters, Bernie thought. The fat bitch. Barbara looked after her kid.

'I reckon I'll go up there right now,' he said, and he unstuck himself from the stool and pulled ineffectually at his faded windcheater. They cheered him as he left. Bernie walked up the hill to the council offices like a man with a mission. He arrived at reception panting beer, and was shown straight in to Athena, which annoyed her, because she was eating a salad roll for lunch. She hated being caught eating, knowing it confirmed in people's minds the belief that her bulk was due to greed.

She covered her mouth with her hand as she spoke. 'Please sit down. What can I do for you?'

Bernie was awkward now, without his spectators, surrounded by filing cabinets and pinboards.

'I wanted to ask, to enquire, I thought I might be the bloke you were looking for . . . for the town crier.'

Athena looked at him. How was it, she thought, that the handsome football captain of Barbara's youth could have deteriorated so fast? It was hard to imagine this man being violent. He was such a teddy bear, so obviously easily intimidated. And yet . . . she imagined him in costume, his red face looming over the frilled collar. Bernie would make a perfect town crier. Strange, she thought, that the physical type should be so right, when the culture was so wrong.

Besides, they hadn't had any other applicants.

'Do you know what's involved?'

'Er, no, not really.'

'Well, on special occasions, or on long weekends, or around Christmas, we dress you — the town crier — up in all the gear, and he goes round ringing a bell and telling people about what there is to do in Newera. Answering any questions, giving directions, being a bit of a clown, a bit of an ambassador.' She paused. 'It would be nearly all on weekends, but we'd be able to let you know well in advance. And of course the tourist association would cover the cost of the costume.'

Bernie shifted in his chair. He was wondering how to raise the topic of Barbara.

'Is there a wage?'

'The local businesses are kicking in to provide a small honorarium. Not very much. About a thousand dollars a year. It's really a volunteer post.'

'Well, I'll do it,' he said.

'Um, we'll have to consult the council of course,' Athena said. 'It's really very generous of you to volunteer your time. I'll give you a ring in the next few days if you like.' She stopped talking, and looked at him in a way that made it clear he was expected to leave.

Bernie stood, shifting his weight from one thong to the other.

'How's your kid?' he said.

'Good, thanks,' replied Athena with foreboding.

'Barbara still looking after it?'

'Yes.'

Bernie shifted his weight again, as though about to go. 'I really want her back, you know.'

Athena picked up her pen. 'I'm afraid it's none of my affair.'

'You might tell her.'

'I'm sure she knows.'

It wasn't much of an opening, but it was enough for Bernie.

'Then she's talked about me.'

'Look,' said Athena. 'I'm not a counsellor. This really isn't my job. I don't want to get involved.' She looked up at him, and was horrified to see that he was going to cry.

'Look,' she said, standing. 'Why don't you talk to someone about it properly. Someone . . . a counsellor. What about the pastor?'

'We never went to church,' said Bernie, his bottom lip trembling. 'We never did. Not since the wedding. Barbara and me.'

Athena had him by the arm, trying to bustle him out of the office. Her touch, any woman's touch, no matter how unsympathetic, was enough to push him over the edge. He sobbed.

'I'm sure that won't matter. He will want to save your marriage if he can,' Athena said. She was almost pushing him out of the door.

'You're right,' he said, sniffing. 'She'd listen to him. She wouldn't slam the door on the pastor.'

He waved a hand at her and, to her relief, shambled off.

Athena briefly considered ringing Barbara to warn her of the possibility of an impending pastor, but dismissed the thought. It was really not her problem. She took up her pen, and began to write a press release for the local newspaper. She liked doing this sort of thing. She was good at it.

'It's official.' she began. 'Bernie's a crier.' It took her some time to see the unintentional pun.

V

Athena dreamt she was standing by the little white church. On the noticeboard were the words: NEVER TRUST THE RIVER. The sheet of cloud was so close to the roof of the church that Athena feared she would be crushed by the sky. She looked up the highway, hoping to see a truck or a car that would take her away from the impending disaster. Instead, she saw the *Tyrannosaurus rex* coming towards her, paint flaking and jaws bared. She began to run, but could not make headway. Then Sam was running with her. He screamed at her: 'You can't control me. You don't control this. If you love something, let it go.'

'Yes, but how? What does it mean?' she screamed back against the wind, for now a huge gale threatened to blow them apart.

'It means you can't win,' said Sam. 'It's wilderness. Chaos. Death.'

Then they were at the little church again, and the clouds and the dinosaur had gone away. The sky was a cool, remote blue and it was very cold. Athena reached out to Sam, but he dissolved. He could not be caught.

'Do you love me?' she asked, as he faded. 'Do you love me?'

And he smiled as he dissolved and said: 'That's not the question. That's not the question at all.'

Then Athena was in thigh-deep water, sloshing and throbbing. She felt the wilderness enter her heart. She cried with loneliness and cold and frustration. She woke in the darkness, and her cheeks were wet and the blanket had fallen off the bed. Sam was not beside her. She realised, after waiting for him to return, that he must have left her to go to Dawn, and she hid her head in the pillow and cried real tears, her sleepy mind still turning over the dream. What is the question? What is the question?

Sam didn't arrive home in time for breakfast.

The sky began the day a violent orange, but it faded with remarkable speed to grey, pink and blue.

Motherhood had broken a lifetime's routines for Athena. After years of sleeping in until the last possible moment, she had become used to rising early in answer to Jessica's cries. She changed her, and as the sun rose over the river, took her out to the verandah and sat on the old couch as the baby sucked.

This morning there was a mist over the river but, when it was clear, Athena could watch the landscape come awake. It was May, and cool, but still dry, and the river was supporting all the wildlife that came down from the north for the water. A few weeks before, Athena had seen emus swimming across the current, their heads erect, looking like floating haystacks with periscopes. They travelled quite fast, barely drifting with the current, and Athena imagined the mighty reptilian legs pushing away below the surface.

'Look,' she said to Jessica. 'Big bird.' But although the baby was now able to focus, she was too hungry for the breast to care about the slowly moving water.

Were it not for the landscape, Athena would not have liked this time of the morning. The first few moments after waking were all right, but then, like hitting a sore tooth with her tongue, she would think of Sam and of Dawn and the anxious turmoil would begin. The landscape reassured her. It was big and indifferent enough for her. She could feel whatever she had to feel. A cosy, pretty place would have been worse. Sometimes in the mornings, she would cry quietly, feeling the baby draw fluid from her as the saltier stuff flowed from her eyes.

Athena had lived in the Riverland almost a year and a half, and she was beginning to love the landscape. She had seen how quickly the plains would be dusted with green after winter rain — due any day now — and how soon that would change to ochre in summer.

Even when there were no clouds, the sky dominated. Sunsets were unfailingly dramatic, filling the sky with red and purple. Like the sea, the landscape reflected the sky, turning grey, pink, red and golden as the days and the seasons wore on. At night, the sky came closer and weighed heavily on the land, but when there was moonlight, it lifted a little. Still one was mindful of the great milky sweep of stars that hung, it seemed, just overhead, and only just out of reach.

Athena heard Sam's car pull up as she got ready to leave for work. Jessica was almost asleep again, and she cried as Athena, suddenly tense, picked her up.

He came in and looked straight at the child. 'She doesn't like being disturbed,' he said.

Athena felt a wave of fury. He hadn't even said hello.

'Why are you trying to make me feel guilty?' she said. 'I have to keep working if I'm to keep her.'

He shrugged.

'Are you going to stay with her, then? Look after her while I work? Of course not.'

Sam turned away, but she could not let him go so easily.

'Well, are you?'

To her surprise, he turned back towards her, red in the face. He shouted at her, and the shock of this sudden display of emotion was enough to make her jaw drop.

'It's your kid. Your kid. I didn't ask you to have it. You can both piss off if you want.'

She felt the tears ready to fall, but still she couldn't let him be.

'You never do anything for her. Why should you be so worried?'

'That's right,' he said, back under control, 'I never do anything for her. That's the kind of man I am.'

She had lost him. She bundled up Jessica and went out to the car. As she drove to work under the grey sky, she thought to herself that having had a row with him was in itself quite an achievement, so infrequently did he show his emotions, and so distant had they become. There was a breath of panic at that thought, and with an effort, she brought her mind back under control. 'I wonder,' she made herself think, 'I wonder if these clouds hold rain.'

CHAPTER FIVE

THE RUTHLESS GARDENER

I

'Prune in June,' Ken Neil thought to himself. Secateurs in hand, he reached into the bare branches of the apple tree and made a cut, stepping back to let the branchlet fall. He looked at the tree again, head on one side, surveying the summer growth's departures from the perfect chalice he had sculpted over previous Junes. The winter sun was on his back, and he was in his gardening clothes: so old they were a map of his physical habits. He was left-handed, so the fabric over his left pocket was worn, the blue giving way to strands of white like the wear on a bald tyre. He always kneeled on his right knee, and there the denim was patched and had worn again around the patch. When zipping up his fly, he held the fabric taut by grasping his trousers at a spot just below the right thigh. That spot was now a hole. His hands were protected by gardening gloves, and his peach-like face shaded by a floppy hat so ridiculous that it couldn't be worn anywhere but in the garden, where he was alone, and where he was at his best.

'Proon in Jooon,' he caroled to himself. 'Proon in Joooon',. and as he sang and made his well-judged cuts, he remembered a conversation from his dinner party the previous night.

Rosie had been there, with her husband. The other guests were his grandson Alan and his wife, and Athena Masters with her . . . was he her husband? Rosie said not, but they seemed so bound together that Ken found it hard to believe that it was not by matrimony. And there was the child, of course.

He told them he would be pruning today. 'Prune in June,' he said. 'That's how I remember.'

He had been serving cream of leek soup. He had sauteed the leeks and potatoes in butter, poured on stock, and when it was all cooked, pushed the mixture through a sieve and stirred in thick cream. His hands shook as he passed the bowls, and some of the soup spilled on to Athena's forearm, lying fatly across the table. She said nothing through the ensuing fuss with cloths and water. Order was restored and spoons dipped into the thick, fragrant liquid, but the silence had become awkward.

'I wonder,' Alice Neil said in a brave attempt to break the silence, 'what gardeners in England would have said. Not prune in June. Prune in January, I suppose, or in December. Not nearly so easy to remember.'

Her words had fallen into the soup.

Ken paused in his pruning. Why had everyone been so tense? Something between Athena and Sam. Even when they were talking to others, they looked at each other, and all their words had seemed . . . heavy. Loaded. Athena had breast-fed the child in front of them, carrying on conversation as though nothing was happening. If anything, she talked more when her breast was exposed than at other times. The men looked at her when she spoke, tried not to gawp at her balloon of white flesh, then averted their eyes, unsure whether it was ruder to look or not to look at her when she was speaking.

Ken liked to think that the occasion had been a success. The food, after all, had been good. They had eaten everything. He had no leftovers. And yet . . . It was difficult to say. Had they enjoyed themselves? He had tried to talk, to be interesting, but sometimes he felt he bored people, with his reminiscences and talk of gardening. He didn't know about these . . . these social things. He had never been good at them, he told himself. And he turned, once again, to the apple tree.

Ken Neil's garden had saved him from a miserable old age and an early death, and now thoughts of gardening were never far from his mind. He observed changes in the weather in terms of the likelihood of early tomatoes surviving, or broccoli bolting to seed. He had once been embarrassed to realise that he'd spent an hour talking to his daughter-in-law about the success of his compost heap; the steady conversion of rubbish to rich soil, and the merits of different types of manure. Horse manure was too strong to be used neat, he told her. Sheep manure was gentler but full of weed seeds, and fowl manure was weed-free, but so high in nitrogen that it burnt plants if used without first being composted.

Ken Neil was passionate about gardening, yet only five years before the space around his house had been bare clay and red sand, supporting only those weeds that survived without water. There had been a clothes hoist, the remains of an old chook shed and an incinerator. The back yard had been merely something to be walked over between house and car, and something for children and grandchildren and great grandchildren to smack with skipping ropes, impale with cricket wickets and scratch into squares and lines for games of hopscotch. The former Ken Neil had always been too busy to garden, and his wife, Lorna, too wrapped up in the family and all the comings and goings demanded of women attached to the Neil family.

The family fruit block had prospered since the first Alan Neil had been granted his scrap of freehold. It had grown, incorporating those around it as neighbours retired or died without children willing to take up the burden of the land. Now it was a fruit salad block — oranges, stone fruit and grapes all on the one property, insulating the family against a bad year in any one commodity and providing enough work to keep two Neil boys in each generation fully occupied. Ken hadn't wanted to stop running it, but when he was seventy-five, his sons, now middle-aged, had been unable to contain their impatience. With Lorna, they had conspired to push him into retirement.

Everyone had expected Lorna to live the longer. She had been forceful where he was diffident, assertive where he preferred to give way. In all things other than work, she had formed and directed his life, as his mother had done before her. Two months after his retirement, Ken Neil walked into the toilet in the early hours of the morning and found her lying dead. She had fallen forwards while sitting on the toilet.

Her nightdress was hitched up around her waist. A half-expelled turd poked between her buttocks. Her face was pressed against the tiles. His first thought was how cold she must have felt as she died. There was a funeral and lots of fuss, and plenty of family members prepared to bring round meals and console him. He hadn't lacked company in the first few weeks of shock, but no one could give him any hint of what form his life should take now that it was so entirely his own.

He felt a mistake had been made. He should have died first. What he was meant to do, what all the solicitous children and grandchildren and nieces and nephews implicitly expected him to do, was die as sweetly as possible, so he could be remembered sentimentally. This would also minimise the time for reflection about what his life had amounted to.

Ken Neil was not ready to die. He didn't feel old. Living for the first time in a house without a woman he felt younger and more helpless than when he was a child. He woke in the middle of the night and was frightened by the creakings of the house and the hissing of possums, the sloppy plops of the distant river and the bellowing of the trucks. The night was alien. He was alien. A mistake had been made.

His food was cooked for him by daughters-in-law and brought round lukewarm to be heated in the oven. It tasted of nothing. He chewed with effort, as though on sawdust. He spent his evenings watching television and sometimes whole days sitting in a chair staring at dust motes in sunlight, smelling still air, waiting for the weekends when he would be taken out for a drive, or sat in another chair in another house, where people would speak loudly to him about unimportant things, their company sharpening his grief and loneliness.

His sister Rosie called every Sunday to take him to church, which was better than the other outings, but not much. Ken believed in God because nobody had ever suggested he do otherwise, but the Deity seemed to him to be a man, like those in washing-powder commercials, who spoke with great authority but whose message was primarily intended for women.

The crisis had come when Ken's son Alan suggested Ken should leave the big house and move in with him and Alison. Alan was willing to build Ken a granny flat. Although Ken had no convincing arguments against this proposal, it filled him with panic. What was he now but a bundle of memories and knowledge of ordinary things, all of them tied up with the house and the people who had lived in it? He knew the warm-skin smell of his own bed. He knew the spot on the bathroom floor where the water always puddled, and the knack with the taps needed to get a decent hot shower. Even the kitchen table . . . especially the kitchen table, had memories and knowledge attached. Old hands with walnut marks and yellow, square-cut nails and his grandmother's voice, relating family mythology. The words still hung in the air . . . .

'It was so dark, and so cold,' she had said. 'I was looking into the river and thought there could be anything under the surface. Bunyips! Crocodiles!' Her hands had snatched the air in front of their young noses.

'What sort of place were we going to? What would become of us? They gave us tea and we all sang. Some lovely voices among us. I had your father, the little dear, all wrapped up in blankets and we lay down on our luggage. It was so cold, and there were so many shadows.

'Three o'clock in the morning, and they just dumped what we had on the shore because the steamer had to get back, and we were all alone in the bush. There was no shelter, and it was raining. Your father and I camped under a kitchen table that night. Imagine that! And do you know what?'

All the children had heard the story before but they always shook their heads, grinning and wriggling in anticipation of her punchline.

'It was this kitchen table. The very same one!' and she would rap it with her knuckles. 'The very one. Your father spent his first night in Newera sleeping under it.'

It still stood there, on the bright yellow and black linoleum, veteran of a century of scrubbing and bread-making.

Deaths, births and broken hearts, all preserved in a miasma of memory and old voices, in that house, at that table. Ken knew he would lose himself entirely if removed from his home. Captive of his history, who would he be if the house was taken from him, if his mind slipped, if he grew old away from these myths and memories. If he forgot?

It was Rosie who suggested he take up gardening. The idea appealed to his pragmatic nature. More important, a gardening hobby would be another link to the house and an explainable reason for remaining in his own home. Since he saw himself as being an unsentimental man, he declared that he would grow nothing but food. There would be no place in his garden for flowers, or native trees that sucked the water away from under more useful plants. On his first day he dug for hours, only to uncover more clay and stone and sand.

Following the advice of gardening books, he dug in organic matter: manure gathered for free from the local pony club, where it lay in rank dollops on the sketchy grass. In time, he built a compost heap so big it took all his strength to turn it. The making of compost was a slow satisfaction. He was patient, waiting for the mess of straw and weeds and shit to rot down to cloddy soil. Ken liked the thought of it. He thought about it quite a lot.

He read that human urine was good for compost, and he considered keeping a chamber pot and emptying it on the heap, but the thought of what his wife would say stopped him. He heard her voice: 'Disgusting.' And so, when it was quiet at night and his bladder was full, he sometimes went out into the garden with a torch and drew out his soft, old man's penis and pissed on the steaming heap. He knew it wasn't normal, an old man pissing secretly under the moon, but Ken Neil's hold on the normal was loosening.

At first his family was worried at his sudden burst of activity. 'What if you have a fall?' his son Alan said. Old people, thought Ken, never simply fell. They were always said to have 'had a fall'. Gradually, as he cheered up and became more independent, the family came to see his gardening as a good thing.

When he found the first earthworm in a spade of soil, his joy was quite unreasonable. He considered ringing Rosie to tell her of his triumph, but thought: 'They'll think I've gone right round the twist, boasting about a bloody worm.'

By the first summer, the soil was good enough to support tomatoes and basil and pumpkins and onions. He found if he fried the onions in butter with tomatoes and basil, they made a dish so savoury and succulent he could hardly believe he had cooked it. He harvested the pumpkins in autumn, boiled some for his dinner and was delighted with the sweet taste of the flesh. He ate alone with warm satisfaction.

Ken Neil had never learned to cook, beyond grilling himself a chop if Lorna was away or ill. Now, his garden led him to culinary experiments. He woke one morning and thought of turnips. It was winter, and time to plant some, but what were turnips used for? He had no idea. He searched the local library for cookery books. Untainted by habit or prejudice, he chose the glossiest, the ones with the most attractive pictures, and cooked exactly as they suggested.

'Good food and good sex go together,' one of the books said in an introduction to a recipe for ratatouille. Ken was puzzled by the statement but provoked into making the dish. He spent hours in preparation: cutting and salting egg-plants, feeling their smooth glossy flesh and the water-filled pulp inside; dicing crisp new zucchini and plumping tomatoes, still warm from the sun, into boiling water so their skins slid off under the pressure of his fingers. The finished dish was redolent with garlic and tomato and olive oil, and yet tasted of so much more than he had put into it. He liked its slipperiness, its chunkiness, and the way the flavor took up all of the space on his tongue. All his life he had eaten meat and vegetables plainly cooked, but these books and his garden led him into a life of sensual delight.

Two years after he began to garden, Ken Neil modified his resolve about only growing food. He declared he would grow only things that either looked good or could be eaten. In his mind, that still excluded most native plants, but allowed in fragrant roses, jonquils, carnations and chrysanthemums, and poppies with long, art-nouveau stems. Wanting to bring these flowers indoors he searched for vases. He selected thin, impractical tubes of glass, easily upset but . . . so elegant!

Now he realised how dusty and drab the house had become. He began to clean regularly. The ornaments and knick-knacks Lorna had bought annoyed him. He got rid of them and bought his own, simpler things. Late in life, Ken Neil began to hunger for beauty.

Pride in his home and in his skill as a cook gave him the courage to invite people for dinner. The family came first, but soon Ken took to inviting almost anyone, people he barely knew or had just met: Athena Masters, for example. He invited them for the pleasure of feeding them. He gave his guests chicken marinated with herbs, pasta with fresh basil sauce, salads made with three different types of lettuce and garnished with a sprinkle of marigold petals. He cut the tips off the dill and sprinkled them on mashed potato. He bottled fruit in brandy and served it with clotted cream. He loved watching his guests eat. Afterwards, when he woke in the night, he knew there had been no mistake.

The garden even grew him a love affair. One Sunday, Rosie had brought around one of her woman friends, newly widowed, after church for coffee and fresh cherry pie. Talking about previous failures with cherry trees — the difficulties of pollination, and how apt one graft was to overwhelm the other — Ken had told them: 'You have to be ruthless with fruit trees. If they don't produce, I rip 'em out and plant another.' He paused. 'It's terrible sometimes, when you've struggled to make something grow, and waited for it, and watched it from a little twig. You get to like it. Then you might have to rip it out, but you've got to be ruthless.'

The woman gave a mock shudder. 'Cor,' she said. 'A ruthless gardener. How thrilling.'

Surprised, Ken realised that she was flirting with him.

He invited her over again, alone, and lavished on her the best he had to offer. He saved her the crispest apples and the sweetest butternut, picked from the vine late in the season. When the turnips were young and tender, he served them to her tossed in butter with leaves of tarragon. He gave her roses with scent so strong you could smell them from across the room, and when she finally came to stay the night, he picked the petals from the most fragrant bushes and put them in a bowl by her side of the bed. Ken was an old man, but vigorous, and with a new delight in touch and taste. Nevertheless, the affair did not endure. His garden was the source of his potency. It had taught him about sensuality, cooking and beauty, but not how to make smart conversation, or sweep people off their feet, or tell them what to do, and his lover wanted all these things from him. Ken was saddened by losing her, but not diminished. He had made another discovery that the working life had denied him. He had wooed her. He was a romantic.

Now, five years after he first put a spade in the soil, the garden was a shock of scent and color against the grey and glossy green of mallee and citrus. By the back door were beds of herbs, which perfumed the air when brushed against or squeezed. Flowers, organised so that something was in bloom all year round, surrounded the house. On the top of the rise in the backyard, where Ken Neil now stood with his secateurs, were the plum, apple, nectarine, peach apricot and almond trees, and a fig tree that bore fruit thick and sweet as jam. Further back were the mandarin and lemon trees now dotted with fruit, shining like little suns, their skins oozing fragrant oil when peeled. The vegetable beds, divided from each other with railway sleepers, were orderly and weedless. The soil was mulched with straw and formed a satisfying clod when grasped in the hand.

In between and around all this ran the watering system: metres of black plastic hosing and sprinklers, each of a calibration designed to deliver precisely the right amount of water to each plant. The system was programmed with a gadget called a Rainmaker, to irrigate only at night, when evaporation was at a minimum and the water could soak under the mulch.

Now Ken made another neat cut with the secateurs. The apple tree was almost orderly again. He reflected again on the night before.

After the soup he had served chicken stuffed with brandied apricots and a bowl of fresh peas with mint. Even he had felt the need to fill the silence, and had found himself reminiscing again, about when he was a schoolboy, and how the teacher's face had dropped when he told her why he had missed the first two days of school.

'Dad had the water, Miss.'

'But Ken, you've missed two days.'

'Yeah. Dad had the water, Miss.'

She had looked puzzled, then concerned. 'And, er, is he better now?'

The water used to come, he explained to his dinner guests, when it was your turn. Whether you were ready or not. It came surging through the concrete channels like a flash flood, flushing dust and straw and desperate, venomous snakes that would wind themselves around anything — a tree, an arm or a leg, to escape the torrent. 'We kids used to rush between the fruit trees making furrows for it to run through. Our clothes were always wet. For forty-eight hours. Then it was someone else's turn. The ground dried out.' He sniffed, and remembered the wet smell sinking back into the earth. 'Now it's just turning on a tap . . . sprinklers and drippers. It's all automatic. We've got the water all the time now.'

'But saltier,' said Sam.

'Yes. Salty.'

And over rhubarb crumble with a choice of cream, custard, or both, they talked about Chinky Basin. Sam had come to the dinner party only because to stay at home would have meant a row, but to his surprise, he found himself taking an interest. He had read the local newspaper's reports of the scheme, and heard Athena talk about it. He had felt uneasy. Now he realised he didn't like the idea.

'We should be proud of this,' Alan Neil said. 'It could put Newera on the map.'

Sam squirmed. He wanted to speak. 'What I don't understand,' he began, and everyone looked at him in surprise. It was his first contribution to the conversation. 'What I don't understand . . . well it's stopping a natural process, right?'

'Yes,' said Alan.

'Well, stopping something natural so we can keep doing something . . . so we can keep irrigating.'

'What are you saying? That we shouldn't do it?'

Sam shrugged.

'What's the alternative?' said Alan. 'What would you have us do, Sam? Give up irrigation? That'd send the country broke. Or let the whole thing die till you can't grow a damn thing here except for mallee?'

'And asparagus,' said Ken.

'What?'

'Asparagus. It likes salt water. Thrives on it.'

'Right. Right, Grandpa. Asparagus.' Alan bit viciously into the crumble, sending crumbs scattering over the tablecloth.

Sam looked down at his crumble, and made furrows in the crust with his spoon. Words struggled to the surface.

'It just seems to me . . . well, it's as though we're always changing things, fighting against the land . . . sort of . . .'

Alan and Athena both spoke at the same time.

'Come on . . .' said Alan.

'Bullshit,' said Athena. She continued. 'We can't afford to be emotional about it. Surely it's a matter of management. Meeting everybody's needs. We can't turn back the clock.'

Sam looked at her with something like hatred, but Alan broke in.

'It'll work,' he said. 'It has to work, unless you all want to pack up your bags. Where'd you be without irrigation, Sam?'

Sam shrugged.

Alan went on: 'Go back to working for a boss I guess. Would you? Home at five, up at seven, wash the car on weekends.'

'No way,' said Sam. 'I came up here to be my own boss.'

Alan laughed. 'Wild horses wouldn't drag you, eh?'

Sam spoke quietly now. 'I intend to be my own man.'

At that point, Ken remembered, Athena had risen from her place so abruptly that everyone thought she was offended. They looked at her in alarm, but she merely crossed the room to pick up Jessica. Coming back to the table, she bared her breast and the child locked on to the nipple.

'I think it's wonderful,' she said, while the men's eyes danced around the room, 'that we can control it this way. Amazing. A real feat.'

Alan turned to Sam again. 'What's the alternative, Sam? What else are we to do, now we're here?'

Sam shrugged again, and there was an awkward silence, which Alan broke. 'So how's the farm going, Sam?'

'Not good.'

'He's always been undercapitalised,' Athena broke in. 'He's never had the money to fix things up and get them working properly. I've offered to help, but he won't have it.'

'The bank's giving you trouble?' asked Alan.

'Not yet,' Sam replied. 'Not yet. I haven't missed any repayments yet.'

'Times are tough.'

'Yes,' said Sam.

'Yes,' said Athena.

This time it had fell to Ken to fend off the descending silence. 'Tough,' he exclaimed. 'It's always been tough.' He paused. 'There is a story . . . I'm not sure when it happened. My father told it to me. So did my grandfather. About the locusts.'

'Go on, Ken,' urged Rosie. 'It's a good story.'

'Do you remember when it happened?' he asked.

'No . . . was it . . . perhaps. No. It happened. I don't know when. A long, yes, a long time ago.' They both knew. The story had always been there.

Ken took up the yarn. 'There was a plague of locusts from the dry land to the north-east, worse than anything ever seen before. They ate everything. They dropped down on to the ground. You walked over them in the town, on the footpaths. They were . . .' he searched for a word, 'crispy.'

And in his mind's eye, Ken saw a locust, up close — the head with its opaque black eyes, like buttons sewn on a doll, the great mealy-looking mandibles, the thorax speckled in black and the thin, hairy legs, tentative as a blind man's stick, and the whole insect cold and alert and menacing, liable to spring. It was as though he had been there. Ken could see it all . . .

'Fires were lit upstream to drive them away. The sky was full of smoke. Hundreds of them drowned in the river and floated downstream in rafts of bodies, an amazing sight, shimmering, you know, as the little beasties struggled. But there were too many. They came in thick clouds. You could hear them. Like . . . like chattering. Just as everything green seemed doomed, there was a miracle.'

He paused. Everyone was listening.

'Flocks of stormbirds flew up the river. They dropped down on the locusts and wiped them out, gobbled them all up. It was . . . extraordinary.' Ridiculously, Ken felt his eyes moisten. It was such a wonderful thing, those birds . . . .

'Then . . . then the birds disappeared again, flying towards the sea. The birds were light grey, wonderful things, and big, like albatross. No one has ever seen anything like them before, or since. They saved Newera.'

Ken was embarrassed. He was almost weeping, and the others could hear his voice wavering.

'Is that true?' said Sam, voice full of wonder. 'Is it a true story?'

Rosie broke in. 'Father used to say it was . . . well . . . a sign.

A sign that even when everything is really awful it was . . . all right. We were meant to be here. God wanted us here.'

Her words embarrassed Ken even more. 'Of course, it may not even be true,' he said. 'I can't remember when it happened. Or if.'

'A myth,' said Athena, dismissively. 'So it's just a myth?'

'Yes,' said Ken, a little defensive now. 'I suppose it is. A white man's myth. About Newera. About here.'

That was the dinner party, Ken thought. The food had been good. And now the apple tree was again shaped like a chalice. 'Proooooon in Joooooon,' Ken Neil sang, and he moved on to the plum.

II

Athena was sitting in the passenger seat of Bruce Pierce's government car, the noise from the road reduced to hum and hiss. They were driving east on their way to Chinky Basin under a sky scattered with bruise-bottomed clouds. Bruce's soft white hands rested on the plaited leather steering-wheel cover and he squinted against the winter sun. They had left late and, in his rush, he had left his sunglasses on his desk, beside the neat piles of paperwork and the leather framed photo of his family, and the little levered clippers he used in idle moments to trim his immaculate nails.

Normally, he and Athena would have had little in common, but in Newera they were both expatriates from the city and so shared a vocabulary. In her company, he was freed from the suspicion of the locals, and from the fear of sounding pretentious which haunted him in all his conversations with Newera residents. Bruce, with his precision and well-ordered life, was neither put off nor drawn by Athena's haughty ways. Since they each worked alone in neighboring offices, they had fallen into an easy, cool companionship cemented by their interest in the Chinky Basin project.

Of course, when she wanted to, Athena could put him on the back foot.

Today he had kept her waiting almost twenty minutes past the appointed time; he'd been delayed by a delegation of local farmers. Athena had seen them file out of his office, grim-faced. A moment later, Bruce appeared at her door and said: 'Sorry about that. Let's get out of this place.' Now, clear of the town, he let go of some of his exasperation.

'Why is it,' he said pushing his arms out straight against the steering-wheel, 'that this salinity issue attracts so many loonies?'

'They were loonies, were they, the people in your office?'

He sighed and relaxed a little. 'No. Not them, I suppose. They're just farmers who own land round Chinky Basin. They're convinced the lake'll raise the water table in the area and wreck their land. They're wrong, of course. The department's bought all the land that's going to be affected. I suppose you can understand why they're worried, but they won't listen to reason. They look at me as though I'm lying to them.'

'So tell me. Who are the real loonies?'

He gave a short, impatient laugh. 'Well. How about this. I had this bloke in my office last week trying to tell me that salinity is all caused by fertilizers, and all this stuff about rising water tables is just a lie put out by the chemical companies, and we've all been bribed to keep quiet.'

'That's pretty good.'

'Then there are the pipe-dreamers. Every time I go into the pub someone tells me we've got it all wrong and what we really need is a pipeline to the sea to take the salty water away. Problem solved.'

'I've heard about that idea,' Athena said. 'Well, wouldn't that solve it?'

'It might. They've even looked into it. But it would literally send the country broke to build it. But they think it's just the politicians being stupid. Then there's another idiot who keeps writing letters to the paper saying salinised land gives off radon gas that makes everyone sleepy and causes car accidents, and there's a conspiracy to keep it quiet.'

She laughed.

'It's not funny. One of his letters even got printed. I had to spend days on the 'phone.'

'Strange that people should be so superstitious about it.'

He shrugged. 'I suppose it's understandable. Farmers see their land dying so gradually. It's insidious. We can't offer them much hope. Seems inexorable. So they feel helpless. And simple solutions are always attractive. They just don't want to believe the information we put out.' He sighed again. 'And of course in bloody parochial little towns like this one rumors spread like nothing on earth. People will believe any bullshit.'

'You still don't like the place, then.'

'Not really, I'm here to do a job. Then — out.'

They had passed the dirt track leading to Sam's farm, and were drawing abreast of the Big Orange, which was closed, since it was a mid-week winter day. Once past the Orange, Bruce slowed the car and turned left on to a dirt track. The red dust rose around them and in seconds everything was coated with a layer of finest grit.

'We need rain to settle this bull-dust,' he said.

'Everyone needs rain. It's late this year.'

'Anything in these clouds you reckon?'

'Perhaps.'

They were silent for a while.

'I'm really getting to like it here,' she said. 'I like the river in the mornings. And the silence. And some of the people, even.'

'Not like me.' He paused. 'I know I'm an Australian,' he said. 'I feel Australian, but I really don't like all this red-heart stuff. I suppose I'm just one of those Australians who only feels at home in cities. On the wet edges. But when I went to Europe after university, I didn't feel at home there either. Even in the wildest parts, it didn't really feel like I was in the country. It all felt like a garden. The rivers were all like canals.'

'I thought you had this river pretty well sewn up,' Athena said. On Bruce's office wall she had seen the weekly notifications of how much water would be released from the reservoirs and lakes upstream, and the effect this would have on the river levels at each town.

'Yeah. But it's different.' He waved a hand at the silence outside the car. 'But here . . . I don't like the feeling that it's big and hostile and I could die out there. I don't like the feeling that it might swallow me up. I don't belong here, and I know it.'

Now they were out of sight of the highway, and travelling across the gently undulating sandhills. The track stretched ahead to the next rise. All around was pink road, fawn stubble and cloudy sky. It was big, Athena thought, and a bit intimidating. Like the sea.

'Do you like the sea?' she asked.

'No one who grew up in Sydney could fail to like the sea.'

'But don't you feel that that might swallow you up? It's the same sort of bigness.'

'No. No, I don't. Perhaps what I like is watching it crash in and knowing that I'm on the land and it won't get me. Or swimming in it and knowing that I can come out any time and buy an ice-cream.'

They were silent for a while, both of them a little surprised at the abstract turn of their conversation.

'I suppose,' Athena said, without really intending to, 'it's like the difference between being fond of someone and being in love. You know, that awful point where you lose control, where it starts running you? But you can't get out of it?'

'Err. Ummmm.'

She had made him nervous now, and she was alarmed at how much she had revealed. She took control again.

'Personally I prefer a dip, then an ice-cream,' and she smiled at him suggestively, which put an end to the conversation, and him on the back foot.

The car topped a sandhill and began another unspectacular descent, but this time the dip was greater, the next sandhill further away.

'This is Chinky Basin,' he said. 'You can't see all of it from here. It curves around. It's much bigger. There'll be seven kilometres of water when it's filled.'

He stopped the car. They climbed out into the chill. In the distance, back the way they had come, Athena could just see the top of the Big Orange — a thin crescent of color above the horizon, topped with bright green leaves.

Chinky Basin was a remote spot, invisible from the highway and hard to find unless you knew which tracks to take: not that there was any reason why anyone should wish to stray from the road and river to see it. The only regular visitors were the Newera Speedway Club, and she could see the tracks they had made around and between the few sketches of mallee, skidding and roaring without doing damage to anything other than rabbit burrows and the temporarily punctured silence.

There was no reason why anyone should point out Chinky Basin, or particularly remark upon it. It was just a slightly-deeper-than-normal dimple in the sandhill-ridged plains that ran on and on to the shiny gibber-strewn plains of the Simpson Desert. From where Athena and Bruce stood the sandhills rose on all sides, and the sky stretched from lip to lip. Halfway down one of the sandhills was a deserted bulldozer, skewed insect-like across the sandhill with its shovel stuck out in front of it and resting on the ground.

Athena could see the soil was already salinised. In the centre of the basin, the few stalks of self-sown wheat gave way to bare, hard red sand, which glistened in the sun as though it had been sprayed with oil. The only plants were clumps of saltbush and strange grasses that grew in circles, like pustules or cow pats: an acne scar in the pale pink dimple of the plain. The farmer who owned the basin had watched it become a wasteland that barely returned him the cost of his seed. When the Department of Engineering and Water Supply had approached him about buying the land and compensating him for upgrading the roads through his property, he had grabbed the opportunity with both hands.

In the middle of the scar, set upright in the sand like a mighty rough-cast pillar, was a big concrete pipe. Athena and Bruce walked over to it. The pipe was nearly as tall as she was, and open to the sky. Standing on tiptoe, Athena looked down into it. There was nothing to see except the round concrete wall, disappearing downwards until the light gave out.

'That's the beginning of your lake,' Bruce said, kicking the concrete. 'When we start pumping, the water comes out of this. This is the end of the network that goes all the way back to the bores along the river. About three weeks after that all this will be under water. You could ski on it. Windsurf on it. Whatever.'

Athena turned away from the pipe, and tried to imagine the water glistening between the sandhills.

'The road would have to be upgraded for tourist traffic. And you'd want ablutions blocks and grass on the sandhills,' she said.

He nodded. 'The lot. The council and the department would have to co-operate. The department would be willing. Good public relations.'

'I can make a submission to the council,' she said.

'Good.'

They walked back to the car. Athena was excited. The creation of a lake didn't happen every day, or everywhere, and she was involved in it. What a good job she had now! The first in which she could make things happen. She felt happy, and as Bruce started the car and turned it around, she realised she hadn't thought about Sam for at least half an hour.

'When will you start pumping?' she said.

'About five months,' he said. 'Spring.'

'We should have an opening,' she said. 'Make it an event, when you start pumping, I mean. Will it be a big gush? Will it be spectacular?'

'I don't know,' he said. 'We'd have to do some testing first in any case. We could probably organise a gush, if it would help.'

Athena settled back into her seat. 'Thank you,' she said. 'A gush would be perfect.'

III

The Ngawait were broken on a grey day, when light and sound were muffled by cloud and the air was full of unshed rain. It was nine years since some of them had tried to explain the course of the river to Captain Charles Sturt. He gave them beads and mirrors and axe-heads and sailed on. But now, on this grey day, four hundred Ngawait warriors waited for the drovers — Alexander Buchanan and his men, who were moving along the river flats behind a grey, tumbling sea of sheep backs. Buchanan had travelled that way before, bringing sheep and cattle from New South Wales down the river route to stock the expanding pastures of South Australia: a new, humanitarian colony, founded with no convict stain and having the stated intention of spilling no native blood.

But Buchanan and the other overlanders travelled far from the infant Adelaide bureaucracy, and in the bush there were no laws. They made no payments, and sought no directions. They did not trade, or stop, or listen. They relied on the gun.

'Saw blacks,' Alexander Buchanan wrote in his diary on one of his early trips. 'We kept firing as long as they were in shot. There were five or six killed and a good many wounded.' And the next day he wrote: 'As we were putting the sheep in camp for the night a black was seen in some reeds and the carter fired upon him and killed him.'

The Ngawait were slow to resist invasion. For some years after the new colony was established, their only contact with white men was as travellers who moved on after a short stay. It was assumed that after a while, these strange and troublesome visitors downstream would go back to their own country. Later, word came from downstream that the white men had built a permanent camp, and it was assumed that they would now settle down and behave like other clans, respecting the rights of neighbors.

As the pastoralists fanned out into the bush, Ngawait territory was encroached on by other blacks who had been pushed off their traditional lands. Battles were fought, and unsatisfactorily settled. People from different language groups were pushed together. Disease killed hundreds, and played havoc with family structure. Totem and kinship taboos were broken. The Ngawait's world was slipping into disorder, and at first they felt only confusion.

Then came Buchanan, and others like him, who crossed boundary after boundary without respect or recompense. They shot Ngawait on sight, in the same way they shot rabbits and other vermin. Even more frightening were their flocks of tame meat; huge, obscene oceans of flesh that trampled the ground and left great swathes devoid of anything green. There were far too many of these creatures, yet the white men hunted down and shot any Ngawait who speared one for a meal.

Control was slipping. The universe was dislocated, off-centre. During the summer gatherings, the changes were discussed. People agreed. The white man brought chaos. He caused wilderness. And it was clear that he meant to stay.

So the Ngawait decided to resist the passage of the white men and their rivers of meat. Summer was the only time such action was possible, and the planning went on for months. The river was high, and there were enough fish to allow the mustering and maintenance of a large group of warriors. In December, two parties of drovers, unprepared and lightly armed, were attacked. Some white men were killed. Others fled. The sheep were left behind, and the flocks of quiescent meat allowed the Ngawait to remain together in large groups, armed and ready to continue the resistance into the winter.

Some of the surviving drovers made their way to the outlying settlements, and the pastoralists sent out parties to examine the scenes of the attacks. Dead men lay with their heads and bodies battered with waddies, their entrails and thigh bones removed, their blood, flesh and hair smeared over their skin and on the bark of the red gums. It was horrifying, enraging, frightening. Something, the pastoralists told the Governor, would have to be done.

So now the Ngawait, made confident by their early success, were waiting by the bend in the river for Buchanan, but they did not know that from downstream they were being approached by a party of police, sent out from Adelaide to rescue Buchanan. The police had been bolstered by pastoralists who had insisted on being sworn-in as constables for the occasion. Altogether, there were thirty-two armed men, and with them rode Matthew Moorhouse, His Majesty's Protector of Aborigines, with an Adelaide native to act as his interpreter.

Moorhouse had been sent to see that the Governor's orders were obeyed. The droving party must be protected, but the Aborigines were British subjects, and it would not do to make war upon them. Moorhouse was to act as magistrate, trying and punishing offenders under British law. He rode unarmed, alone and ahead of the party, feeling the brisk wind in his face and watching the shifting light on the cliffs opposite. On the first night out from Adelaide he had addressed his companions, and since then almost none of them had spoken to him. It was essential, he had told them, that the laws be applied equally to black and white. 'We have settled their country,' he had said, 'and scared the animals they fed on, but we have given them better food, and made them British citizens, and Christians too. They must be made to feel the advantages of their new status in the world, and the chance of eternal life.' His companions had stared at him, and later he heard them laugh.

A fish jumped. Moorhouse watched the concentric circles spread out from the liquid disturbance. Then suddenly the air exploded around him. Before he had a chance to think or register the sound of gunfire, he was galloping back towards the main party, already hurtling towards him.

'Buchanan,' yelled the chief constable. 'He's under attack,' and, before Moorhouse could turn his horse, they had passed him and disappeared around the bend in the river.

The floodplain narrowed here, and the ground rose in an escarpment which further upstream became a cliff. A thick wall of rushes at the edge of the water hid the river from view. And now a flood of panicked sheep was stampeding around the bend between the rushes and the escarpment, so frightened by the gunfire that the sight of Moorhouse and his horse did nothing to deter them. They dashed, bleating madly, under his horse's belly and on to the wider floodplain. He urged his horse forward against the flow, and at last he could see around the bend.

A semi-circle of Ngawait warriors, fearsome compared to his blanket-clad charges in Adelaide, was advancing towards a hastily erected barricade of drays and horses defended by half a dozen drovers. In front of him, his own party was galloping across the floodplain towards them, and all around, dashing between the cliff and the reeds, was a maelstrom of panicked, woolly flesh, the bleats blocking out all sound except for gunfire.

A volley of shots from the drovers, and the Ngawait lines were thinned out, but the remainder still advanced, relying on their numbers to get close enough to use their spears and waddies. Then the downstream party was in range. More shots, and the Ngawait turned and realised they were surrounded. Indecision ran along the line like a wave. More shots, and the Ngawait line looked like gapped teeth. The warriors dropped their weapons and ran. Some headed for the escarpment and begin to climb up the orange stone. They were picked off by the drovers. Moorhouse could see the white men whooping at each shot, and now the flood of sheep had passed he could hear their shouts, the sound muffled by the heaviness of the air.

Most of the Ngawait headed for the riverbank to hide in the reeds. The drovers and police dashed after them, and in a moment Moorhouse was alone on the bank with the horses and could see and hear nothing but the thrashing of the rushes, suddenly alive with hunter and hunted. There was a cry, and a shot, and more frantic thrashing. Then another shot, a guttural laugh, and more rustling. Moorhouse was rooted to the spot, staring at the animated wall of green. More shots. How many? It went on for what seemed like hours. More obscene rustling. He saw a plume of blood spray momentarily above the reeds, released from some major artery. Then there was another shot, and a black head dropped out of the green wall and onto the dirt in front of him. The eyes glazed over as he watched. At last, Moorhouse's tongue came unstuck. He shouted into the wall of reeds: 'Stop. I order you to stop. Take prisoners. No more killing.'

There was a pause. For a moment the rushes were still, listening. Then there was a laugh, another shot, and the awful movement began again.

It was not Moorhouse, but Buchanan, who finally called off the men, and then not because he was tired of the killing but because the sheep needed mustering before they wandered too far over the broader river flats around the bend. At his order, the men emerged from the reeds and leapt on their horses. They dashed off, leaving Moorhouse alone again in silence punctuated by their distant whoops and cheers. After twenty minutes, Buchanan rode back with more than sheep. He drove before him three Ngawait men, their chests scored with initiation scars, and a girl wrapped in a possum-skin rug. They panted. Their skins were matt with dust and they smelt of fear.

'Here's your prisoners, Mister,' said Buchanan. The blacks crouched in the dust at the horse's feet.

That night, the party camped a little downstream, closer to Adelaide and away from the corpses and blood in the rushes. It would have been a moonlit night, but the blanket of cloud that had covered them all day shielded them from the harsh gaze of the stars. The only light came from the fires; outside the rings of amber light, the sea of sheep nudged and pushed all around them. Moorhouse sat apart, then went to check on the prisoners, left under the guard of one of the constables. As he approached, he caught sight of a man's feet on the edge of the circle of firelight. As he watched, trousers dropped over the boots.

'What's going on?' Moorhouse shouted, beginning to run. Then he saw the woman on the sand, her legs splayed open on the dirt. The man descended out of the darkness and on to her.

'Stop. Stop,' Moorhouse shouted. He looked about frantically for the constable, and saw instead Buchanan coming towards him out of the dark, buckling his trousers. The other drover thrust into her with hunger and contempt. Her body was pushed along the sand by the force of his thrusts, and the sand rasped: a soft, whooshing sound: whoosh, whoosh, followed by a grunt, and somewhere in the darkness, the worried bleating of sheep.

'Stop. I order you to stop. Animals!'

'There's no law against it, you know,' said Buchanan.

'There is. There is.'

'Not out here there isn't.'

'How many of you, for God's sake?' said Moorhouse. 'How many of you?'

Buchanan grinned. 'It's a grand country, isn't it? And a grand night,' he said. 'Don't you love it? I love it!'

'Love?' gasped Moorhouse. 'You call it love!'

*

Eventually, of course, there was an inquiry into the battle with the Ngawait. Humanitarian sentiment in Adelaide demanded it. Moorhouse told the inquiry that he had released the woman prisoner as a symbol of white man's mercy, and so she could carry news of the white man's power back to her tribe. He did not tell the truth: that he had released her because he could think of no way of protecting her from constant rape. No one mentioned the rape to the inquiry.

Moorhouse said that before he let her go he had lectured her, through the interpreter, on what she should say to her people. 'You should learn two lessons from these events,' he claimed to have said. 'The immense superiority of the white man over the black in his movements of defence, and second that the destruction of life which took place was not to gratify a destructive propensity, but to protect that property which the black man wished unlawfully to obtain. The white man has shown as much leniency as could be expected. Should you at any future time meet with outrage or insult from white men, I advise you, as your protector and your friend, not to attempt your own defence. The government has promised to listen to any charges you may have to prefer, and for all aggression against your rights you are promised immediate and satisfactory redress.'

So the woman was let go, and the other prisoners, the white men and the moving sea of flesh continued to Adelaide.

Some people called for Moorhouse to resign, since on his own evidence of the killings he had failed to protect the Ngawait. But the inquiry ended by agreeing with Moorhouse's argument: the party's behavior was justified and for the long-term good of all Aborigines living adjacent to stock routes. The Murray people, the inquiry reported, had learned a lesson. 'The moral power of civilisation is omnipotent, and their hostility can bear no fruit.'

IV

In the grey hours of the morning Dawn stirred, feeling the itching around her vagina which, due to persistent thrush, usually followed a fuck. She reached a hand out across the bed. There he was: Sam, the covers tossed back from his chest, his hands behind his head. It was not the posture of someone asleep, or of someone who expected to be able to fall asleep. Dawn opened her eyes and put her hand on his chest, feeling the hairs compress under her palm. She moved her fingers down to his penis. There was no response.

'What is it?' she asked. He turned his head towards her.

'Nothing.'

'Can't you sleep? How long have you been awake?'

'Hours. I always wake up early now.'

'And you can't get back to sleep?'

'No.'

'I was like that. When I was depressed,' she said. 'My social worker said it's very common in depression. They always look for it.'

There was silence for a while, and then Sam said: 'Then I suppose I'm depressed.'

The answer surprised her. It was certainly the most self-revealing thing he had ever said to her. She moved her hand up and down on his chest. Do I want to know more? she asked herself.

'Is it the farm? Money?'

'Yes.'

'And Athena?'

A longer pause this time. 'Yes.'

Dawn was unsure how to go on, how to get him to say more than yes or no.

'Are you two going to break up?' she asked.

There was no answer. Sam lay blinking at the ceiling, but under her hand his body grew tense.

'Because if you are . . .'

'Don't. No.' It didn't sound like his voice.

'Okay. It's okay, mate.' She eased her body closer to him. He felt her cool flesh — the bones so close to the surface.

'Are things very bad on the farm?'

'I haven't paid the water bill. I can't make the next payment on the mortgage. I can't afford to buy seed, even if the rain did come.'

'Oh.'

'Athena wants to help. She's got a job. She's got money.'

'Oh. Well then.'

There was a long silence. Dawn was just dropping off to sleep again when she heard a long, low, anguished moan. She tried to take him in her arms. For a few minutes he relaxed, his head on her shoulder. Then he was on his feet, pulling on his jeans, the loose change in the pocket rattling with his haste.

'Rabbits,' he said. 'It's dawn. I'm going to shoot rabbits.'

When he had gone, Dawn got up to go to the toilet. Sitting on the cold plastic seat, she leant forward, putting her head between her knees and staring at the bathroom tiles. She noticed the grit in the crevices — little white specks and black dust.

'Poor bugger,' she whispered.

She had long since given up the faint hope that she and Sam might become more to each other than sexual companions. It hadn't been much of a hope, and she had not invested much in it. Dawn had almost broken the habit of hope. Now Sam was in trouble, and she had no basis from which to help him, even if she wanted to. She sighed, straightened up and padded herself dry with toilet paper, so as not to spread the thrush.

On the way back to bed, she paused at Matthew's door and saw him sleeping, his bed surrounded by a litter of brittle plastic toys. It was Sunday. In a few hours, it would be time for her to take him to church.

'Something to fall back on,' she thought. 'He'll always have something to fall back on. He won't feel alone.'

*

Athena woke up that Sunday morning and was instantly aware that Sam had not been home. When none of the rules work, Athena thought, what is there left but chaos? In books and magazines on the topic, she had always read that communication was the key to success in personal relationships. But now, with Sam, her attempts to communicate only made things worse. She would pursue him. He would evade capture.

'You look glum,' she would say.

'Do I?'

'Are you?'

'I don't know.'

And there was no getting past that. It was almost comical, the dialogue between them.

She would ask: 'What are you thinking?'

And he would reply 'A mish-mash.'

'Tell me part of the mish-mash.'

And he would say he had been wondering how much that tractor part would cost, or when the rain would come, or something of that sort.

She should have left him alone, of course. She should have withdrawn a little, allowed him some space, let him go. But she could not. After a while she would ask: 'Is that all you're thinking?', and the weary chase would begin again, until he withdrew altogether, and she found it harder and harder to engage him.

Athena lay in bed and thought of Barbara. How was it, that with so much more to lose, Barbara had had no hesitation in asking her lover of a few nights to leave his wife? Where did that kind of courage come from? The audacity. Lying there, Athena came to a decision. She had had enough. Sam must be waylaid, captured. His retreat must be cut off. She must have him.

Sam came home in the middle of the morning, carrying his rifle and looking as though he hadn't slept. Outside the sky was covered in cloud, and once or twice during the morning the tin roof had pinged with a scatter of raindrops. She was sitting in the living room in front of the heater with her feet up. She was sewing one of her padded photo frames. On the table by her side were the materials: paisley cotton, lace, thread and nylon padding. When he walked in, she had a row of pins firmly clamped between her lips. She was slip-stitching a hem, pulling the material tight and taking care to let none of her needlework show on the surface. She glanced up. Sam walked past her and sat down on the vinyl couch by the curtained window. He picked up a three-day-old newspaper and pretended to read. The air felt like thick custard. She sewed. Stitch stitch stitch, each one the same size, none of them showing on the surface. When she reached the end of the row, she removed the pins from her mouth and stabbed them into the pincushion. She had made the pincushion herself. The stuffing was steel wool, which was meant to keep the pins sharp and rid them of rust. They made a soft, steely whoosh as she drove them home with the ball of her thumb. Whoosh. Whoosh. Whoosh.

'You've been with Dawn,' she said.

'Yes.' He didn't lower the newspaper.

'I didn't sleep well,' she said.

'Mmmmmm.' Then, when the silence grew too thick to bear: 'Why not?'

She shrugged. 'Who knows. Guilty conscience, perhaps. But you wouldn't know about that.'

The barb was too obvious to snag him. He sighed and turned a page.

Athena stitched away, then lifted up her reel of lace and unwrapped it. She picked up her scissors and cut off a length. Stitch. Stitch. Stitch.

'I want to talk about Dawn,' she said.

He lowered the paper.

'I don't like you going to see her in the middle of the night without telling me. I was worried about you.'

'You don't have to worry about me.'

He rustled the newspaper, but before he could raise it, she said: 'Are you serious about her?'

It was a difficult question. Sam was vaguely aware that his sudden hunger for another woman had had something to do with Athena's pregnancy and a need to assert his independence, to find some ground for himself where she could not intrude. Dawn asked little from him and, in recent months, her undemanding company had been the only sort of comfort he could bear. But he had trouble articulating this even to himself, and could say none of it to Athena.

'I like her.'

Athena unwound more lace. Another long silence. The tension made her want to scream. In the distance, a rooster crowed, and suddenly rain began hammering on the corrugated iron roof. This was more than a shower. Stitch. Stitch. Stitch. The cock crowed again, wetness and misery in its voice.

She took the remaining pins out of her sewing and stuck them with unnecessary force into the pin cushion.

'I believe very strongly in the value of family life,' she said, raising her voice to be heard over the rain.

That got to him. 'Bullshit you do,' he said. 'You're the one who screwed around. You're the one that got pregnant. You wanted an open relationship.'

Ah. Now she had him.

'Having a baby changes things,' she said. She meant it, but was aware that she was using something he could not turn against her. 'And she's your daughter too.'

'You knew the score when you decided to have her.'

'I don't think any woman knows the score entirely.'

The rain came on harder, hammering on the metal. While he sat struggling for words, they both heard the extra slosh of water pouring out of the rainwater tank overflow pipe. For the first time in a year, the tank was full.

'I'm going out,' he said.

He stood up and looked down at her. She was stitching the lace around the inner oval, made to frame some special person's face. Framed in paisley cotton and lace. Contained. Grasped by her stitching.

'You won't even talk to me about it,' she said. 'You won't even talk.'

Stitch. Stitch. Stitch.

Sam reached out and snatched the frame from her and threw it across the room.

'Bloody thing,' he shouted. 'Fucking lace and . . . and . . .' he stopped, stunned by his own anger. Where had it come from?

She stood up, using both her arms to raise her bulk out of the chair. She stood facing him, her fists clenched. She wanted to punch him, to grab hold of his shoulders and shake him. To hurt him any way she could. To make him yield.

'Do you love me?' she said. 'If you don't give her up, I will go. I will leave you. Do you love me?'

Athena was amazed at her own courage. She felt heady with the risk of it all, and at her success in having so provoked him. It was a complete breaking of their silent contract. She had raised the odds, broken the rules.

He stood clenching and unclenching his fists, wanting to run but unable to move. In the bedroom behind them they both heard Jessica stir and start to cry. His heart contracted at the sound.

'Do you love me?' Athena shouted at him. Her hands were itching to shake him.

Sam's head was full of the sound of the hammering rain and of the baby's crying. She would leave him, and take Jessica. He closed his eyes, and heard her shout the words again. He hated it. Her.

'Do you love me?'

'Yes,' he heard himself say. 'Yes, I love you.'

At once, he was overwhelmed by a feeling of impending doom. He glanced up at the ceiling, convinced for a moment that it was going to fall on him.

Athena heard the word 'Yes' and saw his eyes glance upwards. She thought for an awful moment that he was rolling his eyes, sending her up. Then she saw him turn on his heel, almost falling over in panic, and run out of the house into the rain.

Outside he stood for a while, watching the straw in the yard sinking into the mud. How long would it take to rot, now? He walked around to the back of the house and looked over the cliff to the floodplains on the other side of the river. Everything looked newly washed. The air was thick with the smell of water on dry eucalypts and grass. He breathed in deep lungfuls of the rain-scented air and felt fear at the extreme end of each inhalation. What would happen now?

He sat down in the mud on the edge of the cliff. Did he love her? Did he? The words were meaningless. He felt nothing. They were locked together, and he did not have the will to break the bond. He could not see his way forward. It was killing him. And so he would give up Dawn. She had made him. He felt stifled there, sitting in the mud under the watery sky. He saw himself as though on fly paper, stuck to her, being probed, being found out. He couldn't face himself. There was nothing inside, and Athena was about to find that out.

Inside the house, Athena went to pick up Jessica. Her nappy was acrid and wet. Athena changed her. She felt numb, frightened by what she had done. But she had won. He had said it. He had yielded to her.

After two hours, Sam came in and showered away the mud. When he had finished, he went into the bedroom and dressed, and came out carrying Jessica. Athena was stitching another photo frame, the stitches larger now, and less regular.

They were careful of each other for the rest of that day, using Jessica as a shield between them. A few jokes were made, tentative attempts to recapture the sense of fun that had carried them through the early days of their relationship. In the late afternoon, the rain stopped and they went to the top paddock together with Jessica in a pusher. The clouds hung low in the evening sky, a frieze of luminous grey-blue between them and the horizon. The white gum-tree trunks on the flood plain were picked out in the light, as though by photographic trickery. The river was sleek and brown and still, hardly moving.

She said to him: 'I love this landscape, you know.'

'Yes. I know.'

'And I love you,' she said, not looking at him, looking at the view.

And he said: 'You call it love? Is that what it is?'

CHAPTER SIX

LOVE AND THE HEAVY BALLOON

I

Listening to Barbara, Pastor Jones reflected that unfortunately, unhappy marriages did not necessarily convince the partners about the fallibility of human love.

Barbara was saying: 'I married too young. I didn't give myself time. Bernie wasn't the right one for me.'

Pastor Jones nodded sagely. Her voice whined on, resignation mixed with mad hope. He was only half listening, more to the tone than to the facts, waiting for the right moment to intervene.

Rosie Thomas murmured at the pastor's side: 'You poor thing,' she said. 'You poor thing.'

That irritated Pastor Jones. He always preferred to have a woman with him for family counselling. For years Lorna Neil had helped him, holding the hands of battered and deserted wives and dispensing tea, sympathy and words of conventional wisdom. When she died, Mrs Schenke had filled the gap, until rheumatism crippled her. Then Pastor Jones had approached Rosie.

'You have a natural sympathy, Mrs Thomas,' he had said. 'A natural empathy. It's a gift from God. It would be wrong not to use it.'

Since then, he had discovered that Rosie Thomas was indeed sympathetic, but that it was a sympathy without the direction desirable in Christian counselling. Like now. She was all but encouraging Barbara to leave her marriage.

Barbara was saying: 'All I want is a little bit of happiness. I just want to be happy. Is that too much to ask? Would God deny that to me?'

These people, Pastor Jones thought, kept looking for happiness — as though it was the natural state, a right which life had denied them. They never looked for God. And now Barbara had fallen in love again and saw no reason why, with her new man, her life should not be made anew.

In long monogamous marriages like Barbara's, the pastor reflected, the death of love and the growth of bitterness and boredom were too easily explained away as the result of a mistaken match, or as the fault of the other partner. Hardly ever were they accepted as the natural residue of romance, needing work and self-sacrifice and God's help if they were to be overcome. Single people, he thought, were more promiscuous, but more realistic, as though their sins gave them a better knowledge of betrayal and failure and a greater hunger for grace. They expected less. Dawn Bingham, for example — the newest and most unlikely member of his congregation — expected almost nothing of human beings. The Sunday before, standing in the rain outside the church, she had told him about the loss of her latest lover. She had not mentioned his name. Presumably he was married. She had cried a little, but had kept talking though the tears. 'That's life, mate,' she had said to him. 'That's life.'

Barbara had stopped talking, and it was time for him to respond.

'Marriage takes work, Barbara. You can't get rid of your problems by running off with someone else.'

'Bernie *is* my problem,' she replied. 'He is my problem. You know what he's like. Always at the pub. And he hits me. You're not saying that's right.'

'Oh you poor thing,' said Rosie. 'You poor, poor thing.'

'Well, Bernie has to work at it too,' said the pastor, his hand twitching in irritation. 'He's got to learn other ways of dealing with his anger.'

'Angry!' she said. 'What's he got to be angry about? It's me who's got a right to be angry.'

'Well, there's Bob for a start. Don't you think he's got a right to be angry about Bob? You've been unfaithful, Barbara, and Bernie's willing to have you back. He wants to talk. Won't you come to counselling with him? Give it your best?' He paused, but she didn't reply.

'Marriage isn't just something to be tossed aside, Barbara. It's a sacred vow. Won't you go the extra mile?'

Barbara shook her head, and stood up. 'Look. I'm sorry. I didn't ask you to come. You can't help these things you know. People fall in love with someone else. It happens. You can't control it.' She took a puff of her cigarette and put her hand on her hip. 'I just love Bob, and that's all there is to it. We're going to be together. It's like, it's like I've been lifted up . . . I'm not going to come down, back to this. Back to Bernie.'

Pastor Jones nodded. 'When, exactly?'

'What do you mean?'

'When are you going to be together? You say he's going to move out of his home, leave his wife and family. How do you know he will? Men often don't do as they say when it comes down to it, you know.'

'He loves me,' Barbara said. But the pastor had hit on a raw spot and knew it. Barbara was worn out with waiting for her lover's too-infrequent telephone calls. She pitied the anguish in his voice when he talked about leaving his children. She did not yet doubt her lover, but she had said to him: 'I understand you need time but, please, make it as soon as you can 'cos I just can't hack it alone. I just can't hack it alone.'

Bob had been going to move out the month before, but then he had slipped a disc and been physically as well as emotionally paralysed. He had recovered only a week before his daughter's birthday party. That had been last weekend. Barbara was still waiting for the call to tell her to pack her bags and come to Adelaide.

'Human love is very fallible, Barbara,' the pastor was saying. He was gathering his things and standing. Rosie jerked upright beside him. 'If you need something stronger, you know where to find it. And think about Bernie.'

'Thanks,' said Barbara. 'But I'll be fine. And tell Bernie not to bother himself.'

Outside, the rain had stopped for the moment and there were blue holes in the blanketed sky. Rosie watched the red sloppy mud splatter up on to the pastor's polished shoes and thought how hopeless she was at this work, this counselling. She prayed: 'Oh help her, God. I don't know how. What's right? I don't know.'

II

It rained for a week, with a few breaks. When Sam and Athena came home from work, they rushed, heads bowed, to the woodpile and dragged in mallee stumps, slimy with slugs and snails. They stacked the stumps by the open fire to dry. The snails closed up and sealed their shells. Then they went on the fire, and boiled.

The sand that had shifted underfoot in the paddocks all through the summer and autumn changed to mud, and that mud sustained seed. The weeds around the farmhouse began to grow faster than the chooks could scratch them up, and the backyard was suddenly lush with the bell-shaped flowers and green sappy stems of soursobs: a South African plant, Athena had been told, that had gone wild in Australia and was now a pest. She leaned over the verandah and picked one of the flowers and touched the hollow, bleeding stem to Jessica's lips. The baby sucked, then screamed at the sourness, like pain on her tender palate.

Later that week, the fleshy cactus plants that bound the soil on the slope down to the cliff suddenly burst into a mass of pink and purple daisies. Grass grew. The winter brought life.

It stopped raining at the end of the week, although the clouds continued to blanket the sky and now things were urgent. As soon as the stubble in the paddocks had dried enough not to clog the blades the wheat farmers began to plough and sow, the tractors dragging seed boxes behind them to drop the wheat directly into the freshly churned earth. There was no time to waste. This rain had been a long time coming, and it was already late.

Sam needed money more than time and so he hired himself out to Rosie and Dan Thomas as a laborer, driving the tractor during the day while Dan slept. He rose before dawn. Often he had had only a few hours sleep. He went to Jessica's cot, took her back to the double bed and put her beside Athena. Mother and child clamped together instantly both still half asleep, but the milk still flowed.

Then he set out. He passed the church noticeboard just as the sun was beginning to touch the clouds with orange. AS YOU SEW, SO YOU REAP he read as he drove past. And in smaller letters underneath: 'THEY THAT SEW THE WIND SHALL REAP THE WHIRLWIND.'

He didn't notice that 'sow' was misspelt.

By the time the sun was above the horizon, Sam was perched in the tractor in the middle of a flat plain, sandwiched between the cloud-quilted sky and the wet red earth. Up and down, up and down. The tractor was insulated and heated, the engine noise little more than a hum. At first, the view in both directions was the same. Then he noticed the little differences — a sketchy tree on the horizon in one direction, a clump of grass by the fence in the other, and, as the day wore on, he made his own landmark: the sheet of red ploughed earth was first on his left, then on his right as he forged first one way, then the other, and so he knew which direction he was facing in, even when the clouds in front of his eyes closed in and he lost sight of the tree and the grass. Rabbits raced ahead of the tractor blades. Birds rose in front. His mind was numb.

Depression. Deep hopelessness. He was frightened to think, especially of things that made him feel. He didn't play music on the tractor's cassette player; sad songs or happy songs were too much. He couldn't bear the sensation. He was careful about thinking, and about breathing. If he breathed too deep, he could feel the hollowness inside. All his daily contrivances and routines; the getting up, the buttering of toast, the placing and fixing of sprinklers, the smell of yesterday's overalls, the fullness in his bowels and the emptiness afterwards, the conversations, the love-making, the drive to the farm, all the doings of his life, seemed like little growths, lichen and moss, clinging to the skin of a great heavy balloon. The balloon expanded and contracted with each breath, stretching the emptiness inside. It might be punctured at any time, by sharp things.

Simple good things could be sharp, like the smell of coffee, or the warmth of Jessica's body, or the rain, or sex. They overloaded the balloon, disturbed the mosses and the lichens and the moulds. He could feel himself about to blow apart, and that thought was sharp as well and had to be pushed away.

On the good days, Sam tried to analyse why he was depressed. It was hard. He had never developed a talent for watching his own thoughts, and had never before felt the need to do so. What was wrong with him? Plenty, he thought. Money. Love. He had told

Athena he loved her. He had made himself vulnerable. What if she should find someone else? Worse, what if she should laugh at him?

Worst of all, what if she should stay with him for the rest of his life?

He shook his head angrily. He didn't feel loving towards her. Sometimes he hated her, wished her harm, liked to see her unhappy and struggling to gain his attention. But he could no longer imagine being without her.

Recently, on the few occasions when he had been able to fall asleep at night, he had woken in the dead of the night aware that he had just taken a great, gasping snort of breath and he would be panting as though he had just run a long way. Sam knew what it was. He knew that he had stopped breathing: for how long, it was hard to say. When Athena's will was turned away from him, as it was more often now he had yielded to her, his own desire to live was insufficient to keep him breathing. Strangely, he had no memories of sex with Athena. Afterwards, he couldn't tell whether it had been good or bad, yet he had the minutest memories of Dawn — the down on her upper lip and the crease of her belly button. With Athena, sex was heavy, a matter of forgetting, like a soft pillow over the face.

Then there was Jessica, who made him angry because she opened him up to pain and risk. What if something should happen to her, or if she should be taken from him? He could not imagine such pain, but he feared it.

He should be able to deal with it all, he thought. Other people had split up and kept in touch with their children. Other people had lost a farm. What was wrong with him? He should be able to come through this, be strong. But once he had mentally gone over his problems, and faced them, and filed the thoughts away, still he felt the nameless horror, the nothingness at the centre of the balloon. There was no solid ground inside. He was not strong, and he felt the heaviness, the mind-sapping control, of Athena overcome him and it would not let him go. The strain of resuming control over his own life was too much for him.

Up and down, up and down under the clouds, and sometimes there was a spot or two of rain and he had to put on the windscreen wipers. Across and back they went, squealing when it was dry again and he had forgotten to switch them off. He could no longer see the sketchy tree, or the clump of grass, or anything except the furrows he had made on one side, and the unploughed land ahead. He was on an island of red in a miasma of grey, travelling; but never seeing any further ahead.

III

The bus tore south-westward down the highway towards the Adelaide Hills. With every kilometre, the scrub grew taller, until it was replaced by proper trees, with proper, polished trunks and branches that joined in creased, polished crooks, like armpits, elbows and crotches.

She had waited for weeks. It seemed like months. But at last the telephone call had come, late on a Saturday night, and Athena would have to find a new babysitter. Barbara was on the Greyhound bus, heading for the city. She was sitting at the rear in an aisle seat, her back to the on-board toilet, in the midst of a ragged group of itinerant fruit-pickers on their way to the city to spend the proceeds of the early spring citrus crop. Next to her, in the window seat, was a man with bright eyes and long hair. He was carrying a big Coca-Cola bottle, but it soon became clear that it contained as much rum as Coke. Across the aisle was someone he knew, a woman with wiry blonde curls and crooked teeth. They were flirting roughly, leaning across Barbara to pass the bottle back and forth, and trading meaningless abuse.

'Aw, piss off, Lester,' the woman said.

'Who are you telling to piss off, bitch?'

'Don't call me a bitch, dickhead.'

'Aw.'

A pillow flew from Lester to the woman, and was returned with equal force. Then the bottle passed, and the banter began again.

Normally, Barbara would have protested and told them off, but today she just smiled and looked out through the smoked glass at the passing landscape.

The bus had begun the long climb up the flank of the Adelaide Hills, the plain enlarging behind with the elevation, as though they were lifting out of water and only now able to see the ocean vastness. Barbara sighed, and tears came to her eyes. She was being lifted up, up to the heavens, leaving the earthly, hopeless, difficult things behind. Then they were into the folds of the Barossa, and the trees were big eucalypts, broad and thick enough to shade the bluestone houses and to screen the police cars that waited in lay-bys to catch unwary speeders. The paddocks were recently ploughed and dusted with the first green of wheat. The grape vines had been pruned over the winter months and were strung across the hills in wired rows of recurring trunk and branch, like the patterns schoolchildren made in exercise books when learning to join up letters. Grey tendrils were just beginning to burst with untidy green, and the stone-fruit trees, pruned into the shape of wine glasses, were covered in blossom.

Soon, Barbara thought, it would be parching dry at Newera, and the wise would wear sunblock to protect themselves from the cruel light of the sky. But she would not be there. She was leaving the river. She felt so light — as though light was actually shining through her. Life was flowing around her and over her. Already the dim, dark, routine days of struggle with Bernie, struggle with money and struggle with children seemed to be behind her.

She thought of Bob. At night, he gave off such warmth, like a great blanket, or an animal. With him, she would be safe. She felt a thrill, like a leap, in her crotch at the thought of his hairy body.

Now the bus was passing through the flat brick-veneer suburbs of Adelaide, bleached by sun and watered green again, divided by the black sweep of double carriageway. Lester was reeling in alcohol-befuddled sexual excitement, grabbing and groping across Barbara's lap, crooning abuse at the woman.

'Yah bitch. Come here. Ya bitch.'

The centre of Adelaide was Sunday-quiet. At first the bus terminal seemed deserted. Sweet wrappers hustled over the bitumen and gathered against the gutter. The occasional car swept past in the over-wide street.

'You right, love?' the bus driver said as he handed her her hastily packed case. 'Sorry about the company.' He nodded at Lester and his woman, who were walking off unsteadily, punching each other on the arm.

She grappled her case into the terminal and sat on a moulded plastic chair. Where was he? Where was Bob? She watched the scatter of people buying potato chips and cheesy snacks. Where was he? The smell of fast food made her stomach churn. The noise of amusement machines hammered at her ears. Everyone looked ugly.

There he was! Standing in the door, scanning the seats. He had seen her. He was dressed in a jumper that looked so rich, so right. He took her in his arms, and she felt her hard little will flow out of her and into him. She bent back in his embrace, against the pressure of his arms, and felt the ground slide beneath her feet, and the sky come closer. She dissolved.

'Oh, I feel like we're one person,' she said, breathless.

He nuzzled her neck. 'Breathe,' he said, meaninglessly. 'Breathe life.'

She breathed in and felt almost too weak to walk alongside him to the car. 'The wind could blow me away,' she thought. 'The sky could fall on me. Anything could be done to me at all.'

Aloud, she said, 'I love you,' and he looked down at her and smiled and said, 'I am a lucky man. And I love you too.'

He took her to the flat. It was an ugly, temporary, furnished place with hard plastic-covered furniture and mean stained cutlery and cooking things. There were dusty venetian blinds at the windows, and the toilet, which she visited immediately, had a green stain where the murky Adelaide water — pumped, Barbara thought, from the river that ran past Newera — had been allowed to sit, unflushed, for too long. None of this worried her. As soon as she got out of the bathroom, he took her in his arms again and she was lost. The hard spring light splintered through the venetians, but her eyes were closed and she was lost, lost, lost.

IV

During the day, Athena prepared for the creation of the Department of Engineering and Water Supply's new lake. It was to be called 'Chinky Waters'. Bruce Pierce and Athena had suggested the name months before, and it had been taken up then spat out again, approved, by the procedures and committees which decided such things. These committees had also agreed, thanks to lobbying, to set a date, albeit an artificial one, when pumping would officially begin. Of course, tests and small pumping operations would occur before the official date, and even afterwards it would be a few days before all the pumps lining the river were switched on. But Athena had wanted to organise an opening party and so a date had been set.

She had advertised for expressions of interest in using the lake as a 'recreational resource' but had received only two letters in return. Someone wanted to run a windsurfing school on weekends, if the council would plant grass and build a toilet block. The proprietor of the Big Orange thought a floating restaurant would be a good idea, but doubted whether there would be the custom to justify it.

'Publicity is essential,' she had told Alan Neil, mixing her metaphors, 'if this lake is going to get off the ground.' And she planned a fête. The day of the fête was to be a Sunday, the fifteenth of October, in the middle of spring, when the weather should be clear and warm. A ribbon would be placed over the concrete orifice, to be cut by the Minister for Water Resources. Afterwards there would be a press conference.

It sounded simple, but there was so much to organise. Marquees and umbrellas for shade; drink stalls to be run by the Lions and Rotary clubs; portable toilets, free of charge from the council; the Newera Brass Band was to play, and the speedway club wanted to use the day to raise money to help them move to their new site. The town crier would have to be there of course. St John's Ambulance. There would have to be drinks and food for the journalists, and pinboards explaining the scheme. They would use that map, she decided, with all the alarming red arrows. It looked good. She laughed at the memory of the shock it had once given her. Silly. There would be bunting and signposts on the road, and a public announcement system.

Athena was working late these days, into the night and on weekends. Sam picked Jessica up from her new babysitter, and cared for her. Athena delighted in seeing her plans all come together. She was amazed at her own ability to name things, to organise and control the movements of ministers, engineers and salty water. She began to feel the anxious breath less often. She was sometimes able to forget about Sam, as she turned the weight of her attention to the larger battle for control. He had stopped pulling away. He had given up the fight. He was now the one who breathed carefully.

In the last days of August, she drafted three press releases on different aspects of the scheme. The first was about its place in the national fight against salinity. 'Environmental landmark in Murray

Darling Basin,' said the headline, and the text told how, thanks to the Chinky Waters scheme, irrigation would remain sustainable. 'Engineering has been harnessed to environmental concerns,' she wrote.

The second press release focused on the lake — 'Chinky Waters — a major new tourism resource' — and gave facts and figures; its size, its depth, its suitability for water-skiing, camping and windsurfing.

The third release was for local consumption only and it told of the fête, and the naming of the lake, and the Minister's visit, and all the other activities planned for the fifteenth. Much to Athena's pride, it was printed word for word in the local newspaper.

Athena ran into Ken Neil outside the craft shop that Saturday. 'See you're calling the place Chinky Waters,' he said.

'Not me. The Department. We suggested it though.'

He nodded, the skin on his neck folding softly on itself. 'Why that?'

'It's the name of the plain, the basin. They found it on old survey maps I think.'

Ken shook his head. 'It had a different name once. My grandfather called it . . . what was it?' He thought for a moment, then shrugged. 'Some Abo name. And too hard to spell, anyway. I like your one better.'

V

Athena dreamt of a silver lake that rose above the red sandhills, menaced the silence, then brimmed over, bringing chaos. She watched the flood from somewhere below the earth. She was in her hole, locked inside the landscape, chewing on the bones of a great bird, the grey feathers falling in her lap.

All the capillaries of the continent were running through her and under her skin, towards the fat, sluggish river. The soil was getting between her fingers, and there was no inside or outside. There were no areas she did not encompass. There was no wilderness. Just her, the globe and the flood.

Then something was at the mouth of her hole. Someone was building a fire, and, like a snail, she was going to fizzle and burn. She roared, and the earth shook. Then she woke up in the dark and lay still while the nightmare receded. She turned on her side, moving a mountain of bedclothes. She backed her body into Sam's, playing spoons as they once had, her big buttocks pressed into the curve of his body, her back to his chest. Like this, she could feel the thudding of his heart.

'I've got him,' she thought, and was reassured, and slipped back into a sleep where it all flowed through her, where there was no inside or outside, no area she did not control. But Sam was wide awake.

VI

Bernie was in his leggings and lace outside the Newera Hotel, standing alongside Bazza the Bunyip. The tourists were looking at them. There were men in shorts, and skinny women in funny-looking jeans. The children all seemed to be fat, and dressed in fluorescent colors that hurt Bernie's hung-over eyes.

Bazza the Bunyip was handing out anti-littering leaflets, and the children took them, then dropped them in the gutters or, if made to by a parent, stuffed them in the orange-shaped litter bins as they walked up the street. It was Orange Week, the official peak of the citrus harvest, and Newera was full of visitors.

Bernie was nervous. This was his first real appearance as town crier, although he had practised several times at smaller, more private functions. He cleared his throat. 'Hear ye, hear ye,' he said.

The stream of tourists faltered and paused. Bazza gave him a sideways glance, and moved a step to one side.

Bernie cleared his throat again. 'Hear ye, hear ye. Ladies and gentlemen, the people of Newera have pleasure in advising you of activities in the area today.

'Free orange juice will be given away at the packing shed from two o'clock onwards. The orange packing shed, ladies and gentlemen, is the largest of its type in the Southern Hemisphere.

'Hear ye, hear ye,' he said again, and walked up and down a little, tolling his bell. A small crowd had gathered in front of him. Bazza the Bunyip did not appreciate it. He was walking off up the main street, his tail slapping sulkily behind him.

'Tonight at the Newera Hotel there will be an Orange Festival Disco, entry price only twenty dollars. Be there, or be square, ladies and gentlemen.'

Bernie paused. An elderly woman with pink hair asked him the way to the public toilets. He told her, and she patted him on the arm gratefully. 'Wonderful. Wonderful,' she said.

'Hear ye, Hear ye. Don't forget to visit the largest orange in the world, ladies and gentlemen, just ten kilometres east on the highway.'

He rang his bell again, and used the corner of his notes to scratch his neck where the nylon lace collar was irritating him.

'And in forthcoming events, ladies and gentlemen, the people of Newera invite you to join us again next month for the gala opening of the largest salinity-mitigation scheme in the continent, CHINKY WATERS. This amazing feat of engineering will be opened by the Honourable Mr Phillip Bart, Minister for Water Resources, on Sunday fifteenth of October at a special fête and garden party. Everyone is welcome.'

Bernie turned back to the first page in his notebook then walked up and down ringing his bell for a while. He wished Barbara was there to see him. For the first time in months, he felt he was not such a bad bloke.

VII

The sun struck the front of the block of flats full-on in the early morning. Long before the occupants were awake, the cheap little living area with its formica breakfast bar and nylon carpet was heating up. Barbara always lowered the venetians before going to bed, coaxing the grubby cord past the places where it stuck. But now, at six o'clock, the glare of the day was punching its way through the sags in the slats. Last night's washing up — two saucepans, two plates, two half-drunk mugs of Nescafe, and two vinegary-smelling wine glasses — was stacked in the sink. Bob came out of the bedroom, naked except for a black jockstrap, his stomach and chest looming hairily above his pin-like legs. He thumped down on the settee, and the floor shook, causing the skin on the coffee slops in the sink to wrinkle in strange, mineral patterns. His damp flesh made a farting noise against the vinyl, and he turned his sleep-devastated face from side to side, taking in the smells of washing up and sex, the hole in the carpet by the window, the curly television aerial he had sellotaped to the wall in the hope of better reception. He felt a tear forming in the corner of his eye. He blinked hard, but it remained in place. He blinked again, and it rolled satisfyingly down his face, dropped, and hung like a jewel on the hairs of his chest.

It was two months since he had moved here with Barbara, and now it was just two days until his fortieth birthday. Had he still been at home, the house would have been full of whispers as his wife organised a surprise party, which would be no surprise at all. He imagined it: the manufactured excuse to get him out of the house — what would it be? An urgent need for cigarettes? A friend pretending to need help? He imagined his willing connivance, and his return to a darkened room, which would suddenly snap full of light and shouting friends, and Heather with her tight, wry smile. Barbara's family had been less sentimental. They had never made a big thing of birthdays. If she organised a party, it really would be a surprise. In any case, who would she invite? Bob had told Barbara that his marriage was boring. He had left his family because he had fallen in love with the image of himself he saw in Barbara's eyes. Now he was finding that he preferred his surprises to be predictable.

He squished up his eyes again, and felt another tear start its journey down his body. He looked at his chest and saw the drops of salty water hanging on the wilderness of his chest hairs. He shook his body a little, and they sank below view. He had never liked his body hair. Until he met Barbara, he had thought it a turn-off for women, so matted and damp, but she claimed to like it. It would be better, he thought, if he could comb and order it — part it neatly down the middle, like the hair on his head. Surely that would be better?

Early in their living together, over a restaurant table, he had told Barbara that he feared what people would think of him for leaving his family.

'You shouldn't worry what other people think,' she had said, swilling red wine around her glass and surreptitiously, under the table, stroking the hard part at the front of his leg with her foot.

He stared at his fingertips. 'It's caring what other people think that stops me from being a real bastard,' he said. 'Like Bernie. A real fake.' He had liked the way that sounded, but Barbara just put her glass down and licked sediment off her teeth. What he said made no sense to her at all.

Barbara had got a job cleaning an office. She left the flat each afternoon at five, before he got home from work, and would return to find him making attempts to cook for her. He chopped the vegetables timidly, into neat piles of evenly sized pieces. He had a slow, helpless way of peeling a potato.

'What would you do without me?' she would say, bustling in.

Usually he just laughed and slapped her on the bottom and retreated round the breakfast bar to the couch but, one night, just recently, he had said: 'I would go back to my family.' He had seen the words coming out of his mouth, and wanted to snatch them back, but they hung in the air just out of reach. She held the potato tight, as though it was a knot at the end of a rope, and flayed at it with the peeler. Nothing more had been said.

Now Bob got up and went to the refrigerator, opened the door, and saw the cask of wine they had opened the night before. They had only had one glass each. It was nearly full.

Two hours later, Bob arrived on the bed with a crash. Barbara woke up.

'What's wrong?'

'I'm sick. I feel sick.'

She sat up, but before she could look at him properly, he was on his feet again and out of the room. She saw him walk down the corridor towards the living room, swaying from wall to wall and leaving sweat marks on the paint. She followed him. When he reached the living area, there were no walls to support him and he collapsed. She put his head in her still-naked lap. He was crying, and then laughing.

'Oh God,' she said, and hung on to his hand. She thought: He's ill. He's having a . . . a seizure or something. On the way to the 'phone the thought flashed across her mind that she could not call for help because that would mean they would be found — caught doing something wrong, like children wagging school. She had brought him here. She had got him into trouble. She shook her head angrily and rang the doctor. It was only while she sat waiting, his hand in hers, that she noticed the crushed bladder from the wine cask lying on the kitchen counter beside its gutted cardboard box.

'You're drunk,' she said in amazement.

His tears came again. 'I got so depressed,' he said, damp honey eyes looking up at her. 'Don't be angry. I got so depressed.'

How could her hero, her strong, hairy man have laid himself so low? Now she could smell his breath. It was too late to stop the doctor from coming. Barbara met her in the carpark.

'He was just drunk,' she explained, knowing it explained nothing. 'I didn't realise.'

The doctor stared at her.

'He's been under a lot of stress.'

Still that stare.

'He left his wife. For me. To live with me.'

All day in the hot flat, Barbara nursed him, her mouth in a grim line. She was hung between fear and self-disgust. She hadn't noticed, hadn't seen, how much he needed her help. She was too hard. All those years had made her too hard for him. At the same time, she wanted to run away, to have the burden out of her life. For the first time she feared they wouldn't make it together, and the test on which she had set so much store — that he should leave his wife for her — was not the thing that counted after all. He slept, snoring sourly. Every hour or so he woke and called for her like a child. She lay beside him and held him. He was still drunk, of course, but his penis sprang erect as though she had accidentally pressed some small, concealed button or moved a hidden lever. He pushed his hand between her legs and grabbed her roughly, as though not fully aware of what he was doing. Twice, he fell asleep still clutching her most tender parts. In the course of the day, she calculated, they made love half a dozen times, but hardly spoke at all.

Towards evening she opened the blinds and windows to let in the cool air, and he woke properly sober. He felt foolish. He said: 'Thank you. Thank you for being so good to me. That's why. It's because I care for you so much. You mean so much to me, and I haven't been able to say. That is why I was depressed.'

For that night, and for some of the nights that followed, it was a serviceable fiction, and it delayed their descent from the stars.

Then, one evening, Barbara came home from her cleaning job and saw that his car was not in its normal spot. She walked up the stairs slowly, dragging her vacuum cleaner, its pipes knocking hollowly against the thick pastel paint on the breeze-block walls. She opened the door on the fetid smells of the place, the coma of their togetherness. She already knew. All his things were gone. He had even taken the pictures of his children off the pinboard, and replaced the drawing pins so carefully that there were no extra holes. There was no note. She dropped the vacuum cleaner and her bag, and walked up the corridor to the bedroom. His clothes had gone too. In the dust by the built-in wardrobe was a champagne cork kicking around in the hairbrush droppings and the dust. They had drunk the bottle together in bed, and he had said it tasted flinty. Oh, it had been sharp, being together. The champagne cork kicked in the dust. Kick.

She walked back down the corridor again. She wrapped her arms tightly around herself, and walked up and back again, eyes dry, back and forth, trying to eke out the feeling little by little, so it wouldn't blow her away.

*

The bus was almost empty when it made its descent from the hills. Barbara, sitting up the front this time, saw the vast flatness rise up to meet her and the sky retreat overhead. She had been brought back to earth. Bernie, the town crier, would be at the bus station to meet her.

VIII

In the middle of September, Athena heard on the radio that the aurora australis had been seen in the southern skies over the Riverland. That night, she and Sam stood on the verandah of the farmhouse and watched.

Only two evenings before, Athena had seen the full moon rise, fat and orange while close to the horizon and a less portentous disc later in the night. Now there was no moon and no cloud, and the stars dominated. Athena and Sam had switched off the lights in the farmhouse and as her eyes adjusted to the light, Athena's view of the night improved. First there were just dots of light against the black, but as her pupils dilated (she could almost feel the relaxation of the muscles) she saw the milky whiteness between the pinpoints, like a spill of liquid, or a river. Lower down the bowl of night were pools of phosphorescence. These, she realised, were other galaxies. There was Orion, looming in the north over the roof of the farmhouse, and there was the Southern Cross in front of them. Now she could see even better, and it was clear to her that the stars were not all one color. Some were white, others blue and pink. Some seemed to move. It was rare, on a night like this, not to see shooting stars — urgent streaks of light against the stillness, and already Athena had seen so many she had given up making wishes.

Now, with her eyes fully adjusted, she saw other movements — satellites, travelling quickly across the canopy from horizon to horizon, never wavering, rising and falling without fuss. Like busybodies. Like ants. There was so much junk in the sky, she thought, as she followed one across the stillness.

'There,' said Sam, and she stopped craning her neck and looked straight ahead. Pink light was playing in the sky, as though there was a projection screen located somewhere between the earth and the heavens. The light cascaded across the nothingness, winking, wavering, almost vanishing, then coming back.

'It's uncanny, isn't it?' she said.

'Yep.'

'Beautiful.'

'Yep.'

'Is that all you can say?'

He looked at her. 'What's there to say?'

'It makes you feel good to be alive.'

'Or how small we are.'

'Yes.'

They watched the sky in silence for a while, then he said: 'If anything should happen to me . . . When I'm dead, I should, if there's . . . you know. I'd want Jessica to have the farm. To inherit this.'

'Inherit your debts, you mean.'

'I own some of it. You could pay it off. For her, and for you.'

Athena registered that he was talking seriously.

'You love her after all, don't you.'

'Yes. Of course.'

He picked at one of the Athol pine branches that hung over the verandah, broke off one of the long, segmented needles, sniffed it and then tasted it.

'I'd like her to have it,' he said. 'To have the chance . . . to run a bit of land. She might do better with it than me. By the time she grows up, it might be different.'

'Better prices?'

He shook his head. 'Not just that.' He struggled for words, twisting the pine needle in his hand. 'She might like it better. Be happier. Not work so hard. Just let it . . . let it be.'

Athena sniffed. 'And go broke?'

Sam shrugged, dropped the pine needle and went back into the farmhouse.

Left alone, Athena looked up at the sky and saw the stars again. The warm curtains of light had gone, and although the smell and the sound of the land was all around her, the sky was cold and empty, enclosing the planet in an impersonal grip.

On the other side of town, standing under the almond tree in his garden, Ken and Rosie were also watching the display. She and Dan had come to dinner (lamb kebabs marinated in ground almonds, yoghurt and fresh coriander, served with roast pumpkin with raisins in the centre). Dan had fallen asleep, burping softly, in one of Ken's big armchairs, so brother and sister had come out together to watch the sky.

Ken had been giving Rosie the scientific explanation for the aurora. Rosie had not taken it in.

She said: 'It's not really enough, is it? Science, I mean.'

He didn't reply immediately. 'Science tells us why it's happening,' he said at last.

'No. It tells us how. Not why.'

'Then why?'

'God,' she said, with quiet conviction.

He snorted and, although she was usually more articulate than him, she began to stammer.

'Perhaps . . . I mean . . . it's to show us that, that there's someone there. The sky . . . there's someone there. It's not just empty.'

'You mean it's a sign,' he said, mocking her.

'Oh I hope not,' said Rosie. 'I hope not.'

CHAPTER SEVEN

FISH FOOD AND THE VACATED SKY

I

On the day the Ngawait were defeated, Thomas Pelican Short had been a toddler. His father died in the rushes, along with most of his other male relatives. Forty-five years later, Short was living on the mission in a house built out of kerosene tins. He had forgotten his traditional name, and he earned money by collecting horse and sheep dung and selling it for fertiliser. Nevertheless, some of the ancient ways had been passed on to him by the women, and by those men who had been too old to fight. One day, Short managed to convince Kingsford Laws that he knew how to decoy an Australian native duck.

At Law's request, Short spent two weeks camped under the grape vine in his backyard, where he made boomerangs, nulla nullas, spears and a bark canoe in the old way. To start with, he also made the rush baskets and the twine — women's things. Meanwhile, he talked. He told Laws the stories he had been taught as a little boy. Kingsford Laws took notes, then bought the spears and the nulla nullas and sent them off to the South Australian Museum.

One morning, Thomas Pelican Short took the money Laws gave him and walked into Newera. He came back two days later, his eyes hopping and his breath sour with alcohol. Kingsford Laws lectured him.

'He does not seem to understand,' Laws wrote in his journal 'the vital work in which he is involved, for surely it is only in this way that the artifacts of this dying race can be preserved for the scientists of the future.'

The next day, Laws recorded, Short seemed contrite and was willing to start work again. This time he made a basket arrangement out of bark and rushes and stuck bird feathers around the outside. He chewed more rushes and wove the masticated mess into string, and used this to tie the feathered basket to a boomerang.

'When I asked him the purpose of this contraption,' Laws wrote, 'he informed me it was for decoying ducks. The boomerang is hurled through the air with the decoy duck attached, and surrounding ducks are lured to the area. I had Thomas demonstrate the technique to me, and then ventured to try it myself, having been previously instructed by my sable friends in the correct method of throwing the boomerang. The basket arrangement looked most extraordinary as it flew through the air. Surely the ingenuity of these savage people cannot be denied!

'Given the earlier breach in our relations, I made a point of expressing my pleasure to Thomas, and informing him that I would immediately dispatch the duck decoy to the South Australian Museum, the officials of which could not fail to appreciate his skill, and where the duck decoy would be preserved for the instruction of future generations. He seemed delighted by this knowledge, and expressed himself with the child-like enthusiasm which comes so easily to these people, rolling around in the dust, pointing his finger at the decoy duck and laughing mightily.'

Kingsford Laws collected more waddies than digging sticks, more spears than baskets. He took the things that were made and carried by men, assuming them to be more important. Short soon realised he was paid more for producing the warlike and exotic, and he manufactured accordingly. The weapons looked impressive in the museum, where they were displayed in a room just down the corridor from Ancient Egypt, just above the dinosaurs and right next door to the chimpanzees.

Similarly, Laws collected the myths that appealed to him — those with a plot he could understand, or that contained some echo of the creation myth he had been taught as a boy. Sometimes, when these elements were lacking or when he couldn't understand a story, he filled in the details with his own suppositions, blaming Short's recollection for the inconsistencies.

Once the Ngawait's garden died, it was difficult to gain knowledge. Very quickly, words lost their meaning, and new meanings were imposed. Athena never knew what the Ngawait had known. In any case, she was not a person interested in myth.

II

Chinky Waters was opened on the first day of summer heat. Athena knew it was to be so as soon as she woke up. She could smell the warmth: the eucalypt and dry grass and dust, like spice roasting in a dry frying pan.

Standing on the verandah she saw that the river was rising. Upstream, where the cliff gave way to floodplain, the rushes at the water's edge were almost covered. The previous summer's level could be seen from bleached watermarks like collars on the trees. Now they were almost covered again.

Bruce Pierce had warned of this rising water. In a letter published in the *Newera Bugle*, he had said that not all the melted snow and monsoonal rain now swilling westwards could be held back. 'The Department of Engineering and Water Supply intends to allow some inundation of low-lying areas,' he had written. So far there were no floods but most of the water was still half a continent away. It would take another month to reach Newera.

Athena's thighs were already sweating as she stood there on the verandah. This was another sign of summer. In the heat, she moved in constant squalor of wetness, no matter how dry the air. By the end of the day, if she didn't take care, or if she had to walk any distance, her thighs would be chafed raw and caked with dried sweat. She would have to walk slightly bow-legged, like a spastic or John Wayne, and in the evening she would dress her inner thighs with thick Sorbolone cream.

Now she went inside, and tied ribbons to Jessica's pusher. Lifting the baby from her cot, she smeared sunblock on her skin and covered her fair whorl of baby hair with a cotton hat decorated with pink rabbits. Jessica was getting bigger now, and could stand up, if she was supported. Sometimes, her gurgles sounded like words. 'Gov,' she said now. 'Gov. Gov. Mun.'

Athena began to get dressed. Turning to Sam, she said:

'You're not coming? You're sure?' She was sprinkling talcum powder in her bra, to stop the wetness chafing raw marks under her breasts. Then she held up her tent of printed cotton dress and pulled it over her head, fighting her way through the folds.

'No.'

'You'll be all right?' Of course he would be.

'Yes.'

She shoved her feet into sandals, then thought about how hot the sand would be, she kicked them off and went rummaging for her court shoes.

Her feet, Sam saw, were flat-looking underneath, the top of them rising in a slope to meet her ankles. They were more like wedges than feet. The toes were curled up and horny, like fat claws. He supposed it must be the weight bearing down on them. Poor toes.

'What will you do with yourself?' she said. 'It's too hot to work.'

Sam had his plans all worked out, but of course he could hardly tell her. So now he had to shift her attention, slide out from under those heavy, wedge-like feet.

'You'll be careful of the baby, won't you?' he said. 'She'll burn to a crisp in the sun.' He imagined the child baking until she was flat and orange, like a dried apricot.

'I'm not an entirely incompetent mother, you know.' Athena shoved her feet into her shoes, and glared at him. 'Barbara's going to look after her once the minister arrives. She'll keep her in the shade.'

He had escaped. Now she would go. She was not going to stop him. She was too excited about the lake to notice that he was not entirely with her — that he was pulling away from her again.

Athena was running a little late now — not for the opening itself of course, but for her meeting with Bruce and the others and the last-minute preparations. She grabbed her straw hat and piled Jessica out of the screen door and into the car. The collapsed pusher, trailing its ribbons, went into the boot. The steering-wheel was already hot to the touch. As soon as she got in, she felt the sweat begin to collect underneath her on the bucket seat.

Sam came out to see them off. She noticed that. It was so unusual. Perhaps he realised how important today was to her. It was sweet of him to notice. She had hardly been aware of him recently. What a relief that had been, after all the anxiety. He had stopped pulling away from her, but perhaps now she had been neglecting him. On impulse, she got out of the car and walked back to him, took his bare arm and bit him fondly. He didn't pull away.

'Goodbye,' he said.

'Catch ya later.' She swung her hips back into the car, and took off up the dirt track, trailing joy and pink dust.

III

A black air-conditioned car, designed for smooth riding, was cresting the billows of the Adelaide Hills, tyres gripping the grey ribbon that would lead it down and across the plain to Chinky Waters. In the back seat was the Minister for Engineering and Water Supply, Mr Phil Bart, a tall stick-insect of a man, with his briefcase on his lap. The briefcase was brown, and lined with red nylon meant to resemble velvet, It had elastic sleeves in the lid to hold his pens: one blue, one red, one black. In the briefcase were six manila folders, and the seventh, containing the minister's speech, was open on top. The minister's hand was hovering over it like a bird, pen poised to strike.

The minister thought of himself as a man whose life was balanced and rational. His time was judiciously shared between the personal and the professional, the physical and the cerebral. He coached children's football at weekends. He wore shorts in summer with long white socks. He was wearing them now, even though his knees stuck out like eggs halfway down emu necks. He always changed at least a word or two of his speeches, and let his speechwriter know. 'That's a little better, I think,' he would say. But now his speechwriter was back in Adelaide, and Phil Bart was deprived of the satisfaction.

Phil Bart would never be Premier. He had taken a long time to leave teaching and take up politics, and now he had left his run too late. He knew and accepted that he would always be a junior minister, yet it seemed to him that the importance, the elegance, the romance of his department was not fully appreciated. The scheme which he was opening today, for example, had been almost entirely ignored by the media. Of course, it was difficult to explain: a matter of pipes and pumps. How many people even knew that there was water underground? But the concept of it was extraordinary. He was proud of it. Turning back the tide, almost, like King Canute. The minister smiled, and rustled the papers of his speech as he sat, not on a throne on a beach but on the back seat of his air-conditioned metal box, the briefcase balanced on his shiny knees.

Back in Adelaide, the minister had a clean and tidy desk. On it was a sign which he had made after attending a management training course. It said: 'Never come to me with a problem unless you have the solution.' As a result, very few problems were brought to him, and the Department of Engineering and Water Supply churned on in orderly, unstoppable fashion, its advice to him always reasoned and broad-ranging, yet leading in a satisfying way to one inexorable decision. This pleased the minister. He believed in delegation, in personal responsibility and in democracy.

The Chinky Waters scheme, for example, had first been suggested four years ago as one of a number of options for spending the money the other states gave to South Australia as compensation for the salty water they dumped into the river upstream. The options had all been researched and written up in spiral-bound documents which the minister read and on the basis of which he made decisions and recommendations to Cabinet. He had been pleased to see that the minds of his departmental officers were not closed. All options had been considered. One of the columns in the spiral-bound documents even added up the costs of halting irrigation on the Murray River! 'Economic cost: not acceptable. Social cost: not viable' the little boxes said. But all the same, it had been canvassed. That was important.

It was clear, the documents had reluctantly concluded, that the most feasible way of reducing river salinity was to stop the natural flows of salty groundwater. Feasibility studies had been conducted and the department was confident it could be managed. One problem remained. Where was the water to be put, once the landscape had been dewatered? A pipeline to the sea had been plotted and costed and dismissed as too expensive, and so the idea of a disposal basin had been put forward, and, after due consideration, accepted.

Twenty-five sites were considered, and each allocated a letter of the alphabet. Twenty-one were so clearly unsuitable — subject to flooding, or on such porous soil that the water would flow straight back to the river — that it was a wonder to the minister that they had been included at all. Of the remaining four, A, S, V and Y, one was on good farming land that it would have been a pity to waste. Two others were rejected because they were located in the few remaining areas of scrub, the clearing of which, the department advised, would be environmentally regrettable. So Basin S, or Chinky Waters as it was now to be known, had been chosen. It was, of course, the one the engineers had initially favoured, but the minister was pleased to know all other options had been considered.

Even that had not been the end of the matter. The community had been invited to comment, and an environmental impact study conducted. Departmental officers had analysed the vegetation, the birdlife and the wildlife at Basin S. The botanical names had meant nothing to the minister, but he was told it amounted to rabbits, wheat, weeds and a few mallee trees. The only man-made artifacts nearby were the Newera graveyard and the Big Orange. It was true that the graveyard would be subject to rising groundwater levels within a year of the lake being opened, but the council had advised the department that in any case, it intended opening a new graveyard. The gravestones would remain, and no one the department had consulted had been unduly bothered at the thought of waterlogging underneath. As for the Big Orange, the lake would enhance the view from the third-floor gallery.

All interests had been taken into account, all matters considered. So now the minister sat in his air-conditioned car, racing across the unshadowed plains with his pen poised. He struck. He crossed out a sentence and changed the words 'engineering feat' to 'marvel of engineering'. And that image, he thought, of King Canute. Surely that could be used?

'How much further?' he asked the driver, noticing, as he looked up, the dry, bone-like whiteness of the trees.

''Bout an hour,I'd say.'

'Ah. Thanks.'

The minister began to rewrite the last paragraph of his speech.

IV

These things! What did one wear to these things? Although he enjoyed being alone, Ken Neil talked a great deal to himself in his head. His internal voice was an amalgam of all the women who had brought him up and organised him. Their nurturing and their observations (what he had once called their fussing) were in his head whenever he was dealing with matters that they would have seen to.

These things! Since when did Newera have these things? Everyone trooping out to the boondocks. There was nothing there! And such a fuss . . . Crazy. Athena Masters. All this public relations stuff. He'd lose a day. He really ought to put in the early tomatoes, and the egg-plant. Ken Neil carried an image in his head of what his garden ought to look like — weedless, sunny and fruitful, with a place for him to sit and enjoy it all. To him, it seemed that the garden never matched up to his vision, which meant constant work and never having the time to sit.

Alan had asked him to go to this thing. It was an important day for the town, he had said. Ken, as the oldest member of the family, should be introduced to the minister.

So what should he wear? That nice suit? Too formal for thc

middle of nowhere, surely. But then the minister . . . Ken Neil stood at the door of his wardrobe, scratching his whispy grey hair with one hand, his buttocks with the other. What about those nice slacks? A Christmas present from Rosie. And a nice open-necked shirt. And a hat of course. A proper straw hat. He reached into the wardrobe, took the clothes and laid them on the bed. Then he made his way to the bathroom, and turned the taps with that special knack needed to get a good shower.

V

Food for fish. Like most of the words in Sam's head, they were inadequate. They were joking words, meant to denote insignificance. They were not good for chipping away at walls or bridging gaps. Fish food.

Poor Sam. Standing by the screen door, he could feel the heaviness of Athena's feet, and her teeth still on his arm, and the warm wetness of her mouth. The sun was drying him as he stood there and watched her dust subside. He was wearing an old pair of cotton overalls with no underpants or clothes underneath and he could feel the air moving between the fabric and his warm smooth skin.

Those words had been there, sometimes loud, sometimes chasing themselves in a corner, since he made his decision. It was preferable, he had decided, to any other way. Clean. Food for fish.

VI

Dawn and Matthew arrived early at Chinky Basin. There were only a few cars pulled up in the dusty square marked out for parking with string and little plastic flags. The Newera Brass Band was still setting up on its podium of orange packing crates at the foot of the sandhill. The band members were in full uniform — blue jackets with plastic brass buttons and pillbox caps, and they were sweating. Ron Neil, the bank manager and band leader, blew tentatively into the trombone. It gurgled. Puzzled, he turned it round, gazed into its tarnished orifice, then up-ended it and tipped half a litre of water onto the sand.

'Why did the man do that?' said Matthew, gazing up at the flashy metal and navy blue.

'So it would play better. Make a better noise,' said Dawn. 'Come over into the shade. You'll burn. You can listen to them later.'

She took his hand and led him towards the main marquee. There were three tents set up in the space between the sandhill and the pipe. One, for the official party, was roped off but as she passed by, Dawn caught a glimpse of glassware and white linen in the interior gloom. Inside was Rosie in her best floral print, fussing over the white bread sandwiches and the piles of cakes provided by the Country Womens' Association.

The second tent was the biggest one, and for the public. In the middle was a collection of pinboards with explanations of the salinity mitigation scheme. Bruce Pierce, in suit and tie, was standing nervously at the ready to answer questions. Drinks were for sale at each end of the tent, from behind trestle tables. T-shirted men from the Lions Club stood in front of rubbish bins stacked with ice and stubbies of beer. At the other end, an urn, dishes of teabags, coffee, sugar and several leaning towers of lightweight polystyrene cups were arrayed on a plastic tablecloth and presided over by the Apex Club.

Dawn bought Matthew an orange juice and herself a beer, and they went on to the third tent in which the women from the Cobweb craft shop had set up more trestle tables and covered them with their pieces of embroidered linen, their jams and pickles and toilet-roll holders, and their jars of potpourri.

The Newera Speedway Club was selling tickets for the Bash for Cash. For one dollar you could take a long-handled mallet and have a turn at trying to demolish the ancient Vauxhall which sat, pale green against the sand, to one side of the tent. The Vauxhall was painted with peace signs and the words 'hit me'.

More people were arriving — fruit-pickers with rough hands, soft faces and passionate eyes; and a gang of local toughs who stood eying the Vauxhall and drinking beer. So far, no one had hit it. The day was only just beginning to get moving, and already the heat was deadening.

Dawn and Matthew wandered towards the pipe protruding from the sand. A scarlet ribbon was draped awkwardly around its rough exterior. Beside it was a public address system, hired for the day. The microphone and loudspeaker stood gleaming in the sun and an orange power cord trailed off towards the refreshments tent. Dawn stood on tiptoe, her hands gripping the rim of the pipe. She could only just see inside.

'What's in there, Mum?' said Matthew

'Nothing.'

'Let me see.'

'You're too short.'

'Lift me up.'

Dawn sighed and put her stubbie down in the sand, turning it so it would hold steady in a little crater of dust. Then she lifted Matthew onto her shoulders. His hands gripped the side of the pipe. He leant forward. Suddenly his weight was gone from her shoulders. He was holding himself up on his hands, see-sawing back and forth over the orifice, his toes scuffing the concrete.

'Matthew! You'll fall! Shit! Get down from there! Get down from there *now!*'

She could see only the grey seat of his pants and his coltish legs with the socks falling down.

'It's just dark in there, Mum. Dark a long way down,' and he let go and fell back on the sand beside her.

'Matthew!' she yanked him up roughly.

'What's down there Mum? Does anything live down there?'

'Jesus. No. It's just a bloody pipe Matthew. Like the plughole in the bath.'

'Will it suck us down then? Down under the earth?'

Dawn rolled her eyes, and in looking up saw Athena climbing the sandhill above the Newera Brass Band, with her baby in a pusher. She was so fat, Dawn thought. She looked awkward, elephantine, as she toiled upwards, pushing the wheels through the sand.

She grabbed Matthew's hand and started to haul him in the direction of the drinks tent, but he was already distracted by another thought. He was pulling against her, tipping his head back and staring at the sky.

'The sky's very big, Mum,' he said. 'God must like an awful lot of blue.'

VII

Sam had written a note and left it on the kitchen table, and now he was taking a walk around the farm, dwelling here and there to remember how he had worked that piece of land, rivetted that sheet of corrugated iron, and all the times he had walked and driven here before. It seemed cruel to him that he had worked so hard, invested so much of his life in his scrap of land for so little return. That, he thought, was the history of farming in this hostile, ruthless place. He thought of the people who had come before him, and felt with them the weariness of it all: the unrelenting work, the bitterness of never once feeling the land had yielded to cultivation. Why hadn't they given in?

Sam wanted to give in; to let go, and admit he should not have come here. He was weary of the battle. Weary of taking up space.

Somewhere Sam was angry. When he thought about it he could feel the anger, somewhere in his gut. There were no words for it and it had churned there over the last few days while his shoulders moved forward and his face collapsed in on itself and he breathed more shallowly, afraid to take in too much air, lest he fuel it.

Sam felt his life, now, in the movements of his body, which seemed both sad and wonderful to him. He tasted his life in his mouth. He felt it in the movement of air over his body, and as something which coursed through him, and as something which he held in his hands.

VIII

Athena had wanted to see how her work looked, and what it amounted to. The climb had not appeared difficult, but halfway up the dune scrambling crab-like with the sand shifting under her feet and bogging the wheels of the pusher, she almost gave up. Jessica, luckily, was fast asleep, her head lolling from side to side with the ascent. When they reached the top, Athena's body was tickling under rivers of sweat and she took great, panting breaths. She turned round, and was instantly disappointed by how dwarfed the affair was. Bigger crowds were beginning to arrive, and she was not very high up, yet the circle of activity at her feet was dwarfed by the sky and the plain. Far off, towards the Adelaide Hills, she could see sheets of cirrus cloud looking like teased cotton. They were made, she knew, from ice crystals in the highest levels of the atmosphere. That meant a change in the weather would be coming before too long but, for now, the sky over what was to become Chinky Waters was an enamel-hard blue. The Big Orange was half visible like a cardboard cut-out sunset on the horizon and stretching away on all sides were dips and sand dunes marching endlessly across the wheat country, as regular as ribs in a chest.

Athena looked down again, into the basin. The car park was filling up now, and people were moving around in little groups between the pipe and the marquees. The local toughs, fuelled by beer, were tackling the Vauxhall which seemed surprisingly sturdy. She could see them in their tight jeans and black singlets, passing their stubbies to mates to hold and flexing their muscles, then launching into it. She could hear them shout, and the thud of the mallet on metal.

The three marquees, Bruce Pierce had assured her, were far enough back from the pipe not to be inundated before nightfall. It was unlikely that anything more than a large puddle would have formed by midnight, although by this time the following week the arena for the day's events would be under water, and in a year's time Athena's vantage point would be a beach. She imagined the sheets of water pressing down on the land, and the lake, fringed with plantings of fresh little gum trees. She reassured herself. It would be a huge change to the landscape, eventually.

Now she could see Bernie and Barbara arriving. Bernie was in his town crier uniform, lace cascading down his chest. She couldn't hear his bell from here, but there he went, up and down, turning sharply in the dust like a soldier, and some of the little groups of people left the now well-defined trails between tents and pipe to watch him. Barbara spotted Athena and waved, then disappeared into the marquee.

They are like ants, Athena thought, like the ants in the school-yard. Here was an inverted ant-cone, not a pyramid of dust but a bowl, centred on a hole and with the people crawling hither and thither, fussing over objects and each other.

The members of the Newera Brass Band were all in position, and she saw the quick, self-conscious upward beat of the conductor's baton as they began to play 'Colonel Bogey'. The people began to move faster, in time with the music. She glanced backwards over to the other side of the sand dune. In this dip, there was nothing to see. Even the insect sound of the brass band didn't penetrate the silence beyond the bowl.

Turning again, she saw the television crews arrive — three of them, unpacking their station wagons with the weary ease of long familiarity. The cameramen carried their wooden tripods to the pipe opening and set them up in a row. They looked like three high-stepping spiders. Then the crew went off in search of drinks.

Then a big black car topped the rise in the dirt track a kilometre away, and disappeared again into the dip. That would be the minister. It was time she went down. She began her descent into the ant bowl, sometimes shoving the pusher in front of her, sometimes hanging on to it to stop herself from falling. The sand collected in her court shoes and rubbed against her feet. Jessica was still asleep.

IX

Ken Neil stood in the gloom of the official party's tent where he had been conveyed by his grandson, Mayor Alan Neil, who now stood at his elbow. The two men raised their glasses in unison, the family resemblance almost comically apparent, but their eyes did not meet. They talked with the inconsequential toughness of related men who are more fond than close; squinting with practical eyes at the growing crowd in the sun outside.

'Useless land,' Ken said. 'I'll bet the farmer was glad to see the government coming.'

Alan grinned. 'It's pretty stuffed.' They both raised their glasses again. It was only noon, Ken reflected. In this heat, everyone would be legless by the time the damn thing was over.

'It'll look all right,' added Alan, slightly defensively. 'We've got a beautification program. Native trees. Bit of lawn.'

Ken squinted harder into the light, trying to imagine it. He imagined how the gum trees would look in this light — grey and green and blue, shimmering in the sun, flashing red and unexpected shades of yellow. A line from a poem, taught long ago in school, floated through his head: 'million colored gums'. They could look good, in the sun. Perhaps he should plant some natives after all. Along the back fence. It would bring the birds. He thought of the wrens and the galahs that might come.

Athena waddled into the tent, momentarily blocking the light, and Ken roused himself.

'The minister's here,' she said. Quickly, Alan put down his drink, pulled a handkerchief from his pocket and wiped his mouth. His grandfather used the back of his hand to do the same thing, and the three of them walked out into the light.

Phil Bart lept from the car as though spring-loaded. 'Splendid,' he said, as soon as introductions had been concluded. 'Splendid.' He rubbed his hands together and looked around the basin. His eye was caught by the Bash for Cash.

'What have we here?' he said, and he strode towards the Vauxhall, jingling some change in the pocket of his polyester cotton shorts. Bart was pleased with himself. He felt imbued with democratic spirit. They would say, when he was gone, what a knockabout bloke he was — not at all what they had expected. A cameraman from the local paper was following him and he saw with satisfaction that one of the television cameramen had him in shot.

The minister took the mallet. The local toughs stood a few steps back: far enough to separate themselves from him, but not so far as to allow the impression that they were showing respect.

'Well,' said the minister. He hefted the mallet to his shoulder, flexed, then swung it down in the direction of the car, but — what was happening? The mallet missed the car completely, and its weight swung him round.

'Shit!' yelled the toughs as the mallet came with inches of their heads. Over by the tea tent, old ladies in nylon dresses clucked disapprovingly, but smiled surreptitiously over the rims of their polystyrene cups. Athena, standing next to the toughs, saw the mallet coming round again, at waist height now, with Bart hanging on like a frantic crab. She heaved herself backwards, almost tripping over, but gravity prevailed, and there he was, still holding the handle, with the heavy metal head resting in the sand.

'Huh,' said Bart, out of breath and mouth open. 'Not very good I'm afraid.'

'Have another go,' suggested one of the toughs, but Alan was already ushering him away towards the official tent. They disappeared into the gloom momentarily, then Bart was hauled out again by one of the journalists to have his photo taken with the town crier. Bernie held the bell up, its tongue lolled soundlessly and the smile was fixed on his face. The shutter clicked, and the two men unfroze. Bernie walked off again, face beetroot red from the sun, his words drifting after him: 'Hear ye, hear ye . . . New water body created at Newera. Yes ladies and gentlemen, on this very spot in just a few short months there will be water-skiing, boating, every leisure opportunity . . .' The dust rose and gathered on the plastic buckles of his shoes.

'Ya poofta,' jeered the toughs, but Bernie didn't hear them.

The band was playing patriotic tunes, and the crowd was laughing and drinking and the rubbish bins of beer and ice being emptied at a frightening rate. In the official party's tent, the champagne was disappearing at twice the rate planned by the organisers, and more had been sent for.

The minister's head was beginning to swim with heat and hospitality. He waved a blowfly off a platter of smoked oysters on crackers, then picked up a cracker and put it in his mouth. The champagne was really terribly sweet. The fat woman . . . what was her name? Anthea? . . . was drinking faster than he, and sweating more as well, judging by the wet patches under her armpits. She was standing right at his elbow, a little too close, he thought. Invading his personal space. Meanwhile Pastor Jones, to whom the minister had just been introduced, was drinking beer. The minister had made something of a name for himself by being one of Parliament's noted agnostics. The pastor had been looking forward to talking to him, and now, fuelled by alcohol, they were debating the existence of God.

'Personally,' the minister said, 'I have never come across anything that I couldn't explain in humanist terms.'

'What about love?' said Pastor Jones, and the minister put his head on one side, chewing rapidly, appearing to consider the possibility of a mystery at the heart of things. Then he took a swallow of champagne and shook his head.

'We love what we are familiar with. The people we meet . . . those in our social circle. You, for example,' he jabbed a finger at Athena 'are unlikely to fall in love with a Chinaman, or an Aborigine for that matter.'

'And that explains it all?' said the pastor. 'Not just falling in love, but the selfless love? The friendship?'

'For me.'

Athena, who had been gulping the wine, was light-headed. She was at the stage of drunkenness which made her feel as though she was on the brink of some major insight. The light struck the glassware in a beautifully sharp fashion. She sensed depths of meaning behind every phrase and motivations behind the way people spoke. It was clear to her, for example, that the way the men were standing was significant. Both of them, pastor and minister, had a glass in one hand and the other hand hooked in their pockets, their fingers pointing casually to their cocks. This was what it was about then. Who had the biggest cock. Two cocks sizing each other up.

This was a stage of drunkenness she always wished she could

maintain, but only one more drink, she knew, would make her mind dull and sleepy. She sipped slowly now, trying to keep her foothold on this higher plain. Certain of profundity, she decided to interrupt. 'But we don't love the familiar,' she said the words carefully, so as not to slur. 'we love the things we don't know, can't have . . .'

The two men looked at her as though she had intruded. The band was now playing a sweet, familiar tune; 'An English Country Garden'. Out here in the heat. Her mind drifted, and she imagined the roses wilting, the petals drying to a crisp.

'Loving what you can't have . . . don't know. Doesn't sound a happy way to go,' said the minister, smiling gently at her. She was not part of the battle. 'That's the sort of love that dies, surely?'

'Or kills,' said Athena. She wondered why she had said those words. Their meaning — profound, surely — danced in front of her in the gloom of the tent, catching flashes of light from the sun outdoors. But she couldn't grasp it. The men were looking at her as though she were not making sense. She wasn't sure what she had said, and she felt suddenly foolish. Her words meant nothing to her.

'Ah well,' said the minister, and all three of them sipped from their glasses, suddenly aware that they had no idea what they were talking about. The men had unhooked their hands from their pockets. Their arms hung limply by their sides.

Then Alan Neil was upon them, an orange-juice stain on his crisp white shirt, his hands on their elbows, ushering them out into the sun and towards the microphone. The cameramen were standing behind their tripods and the crowd was beginning to gather in a rough circle. Over by the sandhill the town crier was unaware that proceedings were about to begin. Bernie was full of beer and had long since abandoned his script. Now he strode back and forth, his face pillar-box red, ringing the bell.

'Hear ye, hear ye . . . ninth wonder of the world right bang smack on our doorsteps,' he said.

Alan walked to the microphone, flicked a switch and blasted the crowd with a piercing squeal. Men grabbed the speaker and heaved it further away from the microphone, and Alan tried again, with better results.

'Testing testing,' he said. 'Mary had a little lamb . . .'

Athena had dropped back into the crush of people, where the air smelt of perspiration and beer. With the selective attention of the drunk, she was alternately aware of the gossip going on around her, and of the speeches. Behind the marquee, where the portable toilets had been placed, she saw a row of three men, their backs to the crowd, urinating in the sun. We should have got more toilets. she thought. They're all pissed.

The sun, now directly overhead, seemed intolerably hot. It's burning the top of my head, she thought.

She looked up at the sky and her vision filled with blueness. It was impossible to tell whether the blue was a few inches above one's eyes, or a zillion miles away. Then into her field of vision swam a hawk floating like a speck between the earth and heaven. On the hunt, she thought, from the way it was hovering.

The minister had begun his speech, and the people were falling silent. The toughs had been told to lay off the Vauxhall. Bernie, however, was still wandering, his words drifting towards them on the breeze.

'Newera . . . water . . . bloody magnificent . . . Hear ye, hear ye, I'm the bloody town crier . . .'

Athena saw Rosie rushing off to tell him the ceremony had begun.

The camera crews started to film, and the minister adopted his on-camera persona. His smile was unnaturally wide, his movements unusually abrupt and forceful. The whole thing was unreal, as though it was already being watched on that night's television news, the vastness and brightness reduced to the capacity of a square screen. While she watched, the cameramen detached their cameras from the tripods and walked round, taking pictures of the reporters nodding their heads at nothing and writing notes.

'Why do they do that?' Athena asked the woman reporter.

'It gets edited into the story,' she said. 'You need as many pictures as possible. And the shots of us are cut-aways. When you need to edit what he,' she jerked her pen at the minister, 'is saying without having a break in the film, you cut away to a picture of us and do his voice coming over it.'

The minister was saying: 'Today is a most significant day, and if I may say so, very much in the pioneering tradition which saw these settlements established.'

Athena looked up again and saw the hawk, now still and stretched out, as though between panes of glass, or suspended on a string.

'Strange land . . .' said the minister. 'Determination and hard work can overcome. It is popular these days to talk of being green, using the right dishwashing liquid and not damaging the ozone layer . . .' he waved vaguely in the direction of the sky, 'but in the practical tradition of the pioneers, this state has actually done something environmental. To tackle the thing which, and I'm not putting it too highly, is the most serious threat to agriculture in this continent, and particularly in the Murray Darling Basin.

'The Newera Salinity Mitigation scheme is a marvel of environmentally sensitive engineering. You can't,' he paused to smile, 'cuddle it or tie yourself to it, but with it we can make our way of life here sustainable in the long term. We stand like King Canute, commanding the forces of nature, ordering back the tide.'

Now the minister was reaching out with a giant pair of golden scissors towards the scarlet ribbon. It parted, the ends fluttering out in arabesque, then settling to the sand. Then Athena saw Bruce Pierce standing on the edge of the crowd, talking urgently into his radio. The band struck up, Beside Athena, Rosie, like her brother a few minutes before, breathed the words of the song: 'I love a sunburnt country, a land of sweeping plains'

Athena imagined the pumps strung along the river banks beginning to work. In her mind's eye she saw the ancient underground rivers that ran to the cliffs hesitating in their dark liquid flow, then reversing and creeping towards the bores, captured and pumped under the landscape to this orifice in the sand. All eyes were on the pipe, but so far nothing was happening. What, she thought, if there was an airlock in the pipes? Would they knock and bang, as they did in a house? Would the landscape shake? Would they all be thrown off their feet, while the sand boomed at them?

But then without any gush or fuss, muddy liquid, red like the sand, brimmed to the top of the pipe. For a moment it hung in the sun, leaning over the rough edge like a beer gut over a belt, then it dribbled over, darkening the concrete. It stood on the sand for a while in puddles, like water poured on a very dry sponge. Then it disappeared, and the Newera Brass Band struck up the national anthem, pumping it out into the heat-deadened air.

The crowd was thinning out now, going back to the beer tent and the Bash for Cash. The minister was being interviewed. Athena stepped forward and looked at the water brimming over the concrete and sand. Through this network of pipes, she thought, we have connected ourselves with the land. It cannot get away from us now. Now we can stay here. She felt tears coming to her eyes. It was the grog, of course. She looked up again, and saw the hawk, and imagined its puzzlement at this sudden dribbling movement of water in the desert. She felt dizzy. She reeled, as though the earth had moved or the sky had descended on to her. She felt her feet rooted to the ground, as though something had seized them and drawn them down. The country was her body, with the animal pump sending the liquids through, bringing the outside inside, taming the wilderness, making it submit. She reached out and touched the water running down the pipe, and tasted it. It was salty. She held her hand in the reddish, blood-warm flow and knew that now, at this moment, she had a continuous liquid connection with the deep undercurrents, and with the river itself. The land was conquered, had been made to submit. She felt victory, and she thought that she belonged.

X

Now Sam was walking down, below the farmhouse. Once out of sight of the house, the track wheeled to the west and narrowed. Sam walked on.

On a yellow stone, he saw a little lizard. It was not one of the normal geckos that began hatching with the heat, and which, in spring, it was normal to see scurrying away as one walked. This was a fat, pink lizard, of a type he hadn't seen before — no longer than his thumb and with big, bulbous eyes. It looked more like a creature of the night than of this hard, hot day. He crouched and watched it for a while. He had plenty of time. Then he reached out to touch it. To his surprise, it didn't dart away. It was warm on the surface, from the sun, but he could sense the coldness below. Translucent eyelids flickered at him. He straightened and walked on.

The track stopped. Here, just before the river began one of its lazy turns, the cliff was lower, little more than an escarpment, and easily scrambled down. At the foot was a narrow piece of river-grey dirt, littered with the tops of beer bottles and the ashes of fires left by fishermen. Hidden among the reeds, now almost covered by water, was the little dinghy Sam kept for fishing and for maintaining the pump which supplied the house and farm with water. Lying on the bank near the boat, and back from the rushes, was a net filled with limestone rocks. Sam had put it there the week before.

It was cleaner this way. That was the main reason he had decided on it. Food for fish. He had thought of using a gun. He had one. That would have been quicker, perhaps painless but then she would have found his body and Jessica might have seen it. He would have been ugly and bleeding and sightless. Athena would have had his body to cope with. She would have *had* him. Pills would have been worse, being slow and uncertain, and leaving him unaware of the moment of his death. This had seemed best. There was an appeal, as well, to the thought of his death being accomplished by water. He imagined the river filling his lungs, coursing around and inside of him, and he did not fear the choking or the last, spastic struggle.

He waded in among the rushes to get the boat, feeling strange brittle, bone-like things snap under his feet. Other things had died here. Lifting the net full of stones, he threw it into the boat and clambered into it. A pelican took off, alarmed at the commotion. It swept overhead, its wings arched and whispering, its beak stuck out in self-importance.

'So that is what you're doing,' the pelican whispered to Sam. 'Food for fish.'

He rowed out into the river. Although he was in the centre of the stream, he felt himself shadowed from the sun by the golden cliffs, which, with the turn of the river, now rose on the opposite bank. It was quiet here, in their shadow. He lashed the net containing the rocks to his waist.

He sat for a moment, looking at the cliffs and the clear blue sky. Then Sam heaved the net over the side of the boat, and followed it.

He sank to the mud without time for a struggle. His eyes were open, but the water was too green and murky for him to see. He felt his lungs fill, and the slight but irresistible current enclose his body and tug at it gently, like a child at his sleeve.

In Chinky Basin, at the other end of that liquid connection, Athena looked at the sky and saw it vacated. The hovering bird had disappeared.

XI

Sam's suicide note, left on the kitchen table, was not addressed to anyone. Athena found it when she returned from Chinky Waters, her head aching from alcohol and sun. It said:

'Forgive me. I am going to drown myself. In the river. Everything is buggered. It seems best. I have lost the will to live. I haven't the guts. I don't know how I am meant to live. I don't seem to be able to cope any more. I don't belong. Please, let the farm go to Jessica.'

Little words, all of them. They were such little words.

Athena was not the sort to have hysterics. She supposed she must have rung somebody because the next afternoon she found herself watching them drag the river. They found him.

Divers went down and cut his leg free of the net. Athena was watching herself watch them. She was standing on the verandah and she could see their black heads bobbing in the green snaky river. Rosie was with her. It had been agreed, among the women of Newera, that Athena should not be left alone.

'Come inside, dear. You don't have to watch.'

'No,' said Athena. She shook her head after saying the word because she was finding that she couldn't tell when she had spoken aloud and when the words were only in her head. Sometimes she said things very loudly but people didn't hear.

'Leave me alone,' she had shouted earlier. 'It's all my fault. I killed him. I crushed him.' No one had heard her.

'But . . .' said Rosie. Then, 'I'll fetch the baby.'

Jessica was crying, and Rosie had hoped the sound would draw Athena away from the view but she seemed deaf to the child. Now she brought the baby out and put her in her mother's arms. Jessica was nearly a year old now, and big with it. She was beginning to talk.

'Mu . . . Mu . . . Mu,' she said, which might have been for

Mummy. Athena rocked her absent-mindedly, and gazed down at the river.

The divers' heads appeared again, black blobs on green, like those seen in front of the eyes just before vomiting. This time the divers had something with them — a flat, black, floaty thing. Athena turned away. The thing was Sam's body, soft and pallid; prune-like in its casing of rough overalls. But it wasn't Sam. He had gone. He had been washed away by the thick, green snake.

Athena was given sedatives, and she slept. The bedclothes still smelt of his smell. The pillow next to hers still bore the imprint of his head. She reached out to hold, and he slipped away. In her dreams his smell was all around her, as potent as rain.

When she woke, she loathed herself. She gripped and tore at her flesh, at her hair. She couldn't stand the way her body took up space. She was sedated again, and slept.

Later, changing Jessica's nappy, she stopped and gazed into the child's blue eyes.

'Don't let me hurt you,' Athena said. 'Don't let me. Run away from me. Go!'

Who was this child, this little scrap of flesh? Looking down at the utterly dependent child, Athena realised that she didn't know her daughter. She had almost no idea of her personality, or of what sort of person she might become. She hadn't wanted to know. Now, how could she, with her awful, killing ways, be allowed to be a mother?

Grief, Athena discovered, could be very like panic. She dreamt chaos. There she was, lying in bed asleep. Then, somewhere in her head a little shuddering movement began. She tried to stamp it out, but it caught on, infected the things next to it, and they began to move as well. It was a sickening shifting, a fittish rustling, an area of infection, like a spreading bushfire or a palsy. More movement, towering over the bits of her that were still stable and sane. The chaos was engulfing everything. There was no foothold. No place could be found in the awful, draggly, rustling wilderness. And somewhere inside her there was rage, scrabbling for a foothold. Unable to stand and shout, Athena's rage was nevertheless urgent, thrusting, incapacitating, helpless.

XII

The funeral service was held one week after the drowning in the little white church by the highway. The noticeboard said: TRAVEL THE ROAD OF LIFE WITH GOD.

It was a blue day. The land stretched down to the river in shades of grey and aquamarine. Athena thought the mourners looked like figures in a cartoon. It wasn't happening. It was too surreal: these black mourners cut out against the blue sky and the white walls of the church. The trucks raged past. They were not bothered. They were rushing through it all towards bigger things.

Ken and Rosie and Alan were there, and Bernie and Barbara. Dawn and Matthew sat at the back. Sam had been a newcomer, as far as Newera was concerned, and had not been outgoing. He had not known many people.

Athena sat in the front pew in a balloon of black cotton, shifting her weight from buttock to buttock and catching the occasional word from the service, but hearing more of the trucks.

Afterwards, outside the church, Matthew hung from his mother's hand and looked up at the sky. 'It's empty, Mum.'

'What is?'

'The sky's empty today.'

And Dawn began to cry.

The only route to the graveyard was along the highway. The funeral procession, travelling in second gear, forced the trucks to slow, calculate and overtake, their slipstream buffeting the coffin and its wreaths, threatening to dislodge them from the roof of the undertaker's black station wagon. They passed the Big Orange, where Bazza the Bunyip could be seen handing out garbags.

Then the procession turned left and began the journey up and down the ribs of the sand dunes towards the graveyard and Chinky Waters. The track forked, and the road to the graveyard veered up, cresting a dune with a view of the lake, now a glistening lagoon. Then it was down into the graveyard dip, and the silver sheet disappeared from view.

The red soil was heaped up by the side of the grave. It was almost as orange, Athena thought, as the Big Orange itself, and she smiled a little, and giggled. The machine that had done the digging was bright yellow. It was now parked a discreet distance away, yet close to the grave was a pump — chrome green — attached to a thick grey pipe which hung like a fat worm into the grave. Why a pump? Athena thought. Only as they party approached did a workman begin to pack it up.

They gathered about the grave. Words were spoken. What were they? Athena couldn't hear. She could only see the bright, bright colors all around. Then the coffin was lowered into the hole. It rested on the bottom. More words were spoken. Red earth thrown on the lid. Earth to earth. Thump. Ashes to ashes. Red earth. Thump. Dust to dust. Thump. In sure and certain hope . . . .

Then Athena saw why a pump had been necessary. Water was seeping in through the red earth walls of the grave. She heard a whisper behind her. Other people had seen it too. 'It's the lake,' they said, 'Chinky Waters. It's the groundwater.'

Would the water be salty enough to pickle the corpse, she wondered, or would it just rot the timber? Then, suddenly, she was on her knees. Then she was on her face. The earth had reached up and dragged her down, and her voice was hitting the sky in great long, meaningless syllables. 'Ooooaaaaagh. Oooooaaaagh. Oooooaaaagh.' She could not get up. Then people were lifting her.

*

That night the river lay, a warm grey snake, at the foot of the cliff. The stars cut the sky cruelly, and the satellites bustled across the heavens with passionless aplomb. Athena stood in the backyard under the rustling Athol pines and remembered a hundred things about herself and Sam. She had trampled on him, buffeted and slapped him, and allowed him no space. He had not been able to move without her crowding-in, or to feel without her wanting the feeling. She felt sorry for him now, with his softness and shyness and all the haltings and fears she had mistaken for strength. Gentle Sam.

She loathed herself. She looked up at the sky in the hope it would make her feel smaller; less gross. There was no one there, for Athena, in that strange land and that bright garden.

CHAPTER EIGHT

HOPE AND THE SPITEFUL TIDE

I

It was the week before Christmas, the season of goodwill, and the time for the annual Newera Yabby Grand Prix and Christmas pageant. Normally this was the crowning glory of Bazza the Bunyip's year. He led the parade, and was outshone only by Father Christmas, who brought up the rear. This year, Bernie McLachlan had let it be known that he expected to be in the parade as well, and the Bunyip wasn't happy. Alan Neil took the matter up with Bernie.

'I suppose,' he said, eyeing Bernie doubtfully, 'I'm appealing to your good nature. We don't want to lose Bazza. It might be difficult to find . . . there aren't all that many people around who would be willing . . . there aren't many potential bunyips around.' He paused. 'Would you consider not being in the parade?'

Bernie looked offended. 'Don't see why I should. The kids like me better than that bloody green thing. The minister even had his photo taken with me. Where was the bunyip, eh? Where was the bunyip then?'

Alan picked up his pen and pushed it against the blotter, the ink spreading from the tip.

'Bazza points out,' he said, 'that he has always led the parade. It's a traditional thing. People expect it.'

'Traditional,' spat Bernie. 'What's traditional about a bunyip at Christmas time?'

'I don't think cultural consistency is a priority,' Alan said hurriedly. 'Not in the pageant. You could, if you weren't in the parade, have a day off. Enjoy it. You could even race a yabby, if you wanted to. It would save Bazza's feelings.' He paused again. 'You're right about the popularity of the town crier, Bernie. You can afford to be generous.'

Bernie was about to protest, but Alan's words made him pause. He could afford to be generous. He liked the sound of that. In any case, it was clear that Alan's mind was made up. Bernie yielded.

'Okay. Yeah. Anything for peace. I wouldn't want . . . well, we have to look after Bazza's feelings.'

So on the day of the yabby race Bernie was in his normal clothes, and ready to take part.

Racing yabbies were supplied, or contestants could bring their own. The serious contestants held trials to select the fastest from their catch, sending them scuttling up driveways or over kitchen floors. Slower yabbies were culled long before the race and eaten with bread and butter, but the fast ones were kept, fed and trained and in the days before the race, painted with nail polish in their racing colors. The Newera Hotel sponsored the race, donating ten slabs of stubbies for first prize, and five slabs for the runner-up.

The third prize didn't require a sponsor. It consisted of the contestants. At the end of the race, all the yabbies were scooped up and hosed down, the dead and squashed ones weeded out and the remainder put in an esky and presented to the owner of the number three yabby, with the hope that the gruelling training had not made them too tough.

The serious yabby racers were already lining up as Bernie made his way to the top of the hill and the esky of supplied yabbies, presided over by Alan Neil.

'Gidday,' said Bernie. He kicked the esky to make the prospective contestants look lively, then reached cautiously into the crustaceous mass and selected the biggest yabby he could see.

'I'll take this one.'

'You've got to give it a name, so as we know them apart,' said Alan.

Bernie stood, his thonged feet parted, with the yabby in his hand.

'Waddya reckon?' he said.

'Up to you. What about something patriotic?'

Bernie's face cleared. 'Yeah. Call it Onion Free.'

'Onion what?'

'It's patriotic.'

Alan laughed uneasily. 'Okay, okay.'

Alan called for silence. The race would be down the main street, past the Institute and the bakery and the newsagent, with the finish line outside the pub.

'Get ready,' said Alan.

Along the start line, yabby thoraxes were grasped with anxious fingers.

'Get set.'

Claws scrabbled on bitumen.

'Go'.

There was a wild scuttling as the crustacea fanned out. Two yabbies turned around and headed in the wrong direction, around the corner to disappear among the ballet shoes and clod hoppers, fibreglass reindeer and tinsel of the impatiently waiting pageant.

Onion Free moved quickly into the inside lane and tried to hide under a paper bag in the gutter. Bernie gave the paper bag a tentative kick with his thong but got a warning nod from Alan. On the opposite side of the track, a section of the crowd gave way as the middle of the field veered off course and headed towards the onlookers, pincers waving.

'Stop them, stop them,' pleaded the owners of the contestants, but the audience was laughing and screaming. The path was clear, and in a series of delicious plops twenty contestants dropped into the drain and to freedom.

Now there were only four yabbies left. Ron Mitchell, manager of the pub, was racing Newera Champion in an attempt to win back his own beer. His rival was Enterprise, owned by the manager of the bottle shop. Then there was Onion Free and, well back in the field, a yabby decorated with pink nail varnish, now sitting sulkily in the gutter.

Bernie was chasing after his champion when he saw Barbara watching from the sidelines. She gave her cynical, lopsided grin, and he pulled anxiously at his t-shirt, trying to make it cover the overhang of hairy belly and meet the top of his shorts.

Forgetting his belly, Bernie lapsed into his role as town crier, and began to yell out a race commentary. 'And its Newera Champion, ladies and gentleman, but Enterprise is coming up fast and Onion Free is on his tail. Enterprise is sprinting, er, scuttling into the lead. It's Newera. It's Enterprise. They're neck and neck. Claw and claw. Oh bloody hell, what now.'

Enterprise had climbed on top of Newera Champion and bitten off one of his legs. 'Fault,' yelled Ron. 'They're not meant to be eaten yet.' Alan nodded, and Ron and John fell on their yabbies and separated them, but Enterprise refused to move for some moments, content to stand in the middle of the road waving the leg idly above his head. Newera Champion didn't appear to miss his limb, but scuttled into the lead and across the finish line. Enterprise recovered himself and came second, and Onion Free came in third place.

As the winner was announced Bazza the Bunyip rounded the corner at the top of the street stomping his hardest and Bernie, his stomach flopping over his belt, rushed up the street to retrieve his prize, sweeping yabbies, dead and alive, into the esky he had seized from Alan.

That night Bernie and Barbara sat in the kitchen under the fluorescent light. The grand prix contestants, red and boiled, were piled on a sheet of newspaper in front of them. Bernie and Barbara cracked and peeled and sucked in silence, building a second pile of rattling hollow shells.

'Good feed,' Bernie said at last.

'Yeah.' Barbara sucked the flesh out of Onion Free's claw, feeling the splintered shell against her lips.

More silence.

They raised stubbies of beer to their lips, the beads of condensation smudging under their fishy fingers.

Bernie grabbed Enterprise, recognizable from his scarlet painted shell, and began to peel the torso.

'Ya glad to be back?' he said, not looking at her. 'Here with me?'

She shrugged.

He lifted the hammer they were using to crack the claws, and tapped it on the yabby's shell.

'Good to have ya back.' The yabby crunched under the hammer. 'I missed you. I've changed you know.' He burped.

Was it true? Barbara wondered. A few months before he would never have admitted to wanting her. He had been shaken by her leaving, of course, but there was something else. He was more confident, less aggressive. He was town crier. The local paper had run an article on how much his work for tourism was appreciated. In a little, ridiculous way he was town hero again. Now he was looking down at his wet fingers, turning over a corpse.

'You know. I do. I mean. I love you and all that,' he said.

She was silent. She was not going to help him. He struggled on.

'Those times I belted you. I won't. I mean . . . Well, yeah. It won't happen again.'

Barbara stood up and drew the corners of the newspaper together, making a chattering, fragile parcel of the empty shells. Clutching it to her, she opened the screen door with her hip and walked out to the rubbish bin.

She got a whiff of warm garbage as she crushed the parcel in on top. The mosquitoes were homing in on her already, ravenous, sucking her blood and raising her skin in white, strained bubbles. She slapped at one, and got it, and felt the blood slip between her fingers.

Bernie. Rival to a bunyip. So full of himself because he was the only one in town stupid enough to ponce about in lace and a silly hat. Not football or farming or clearing Mallee or anything manly. Nothing that belonged, or had roots, or was sensible or that you could respect. How could she do it? How could she possibly stay here with him?

She saw stretching in front of her a life of low expectations and small comforts, like this feast of shellfish. A beer after a hot day. Sometimes a hug. They'd knock on. Perhaps sometimes a row, or a fuck. It saved having to say hello.

Was this a life she wanted? Could she live it?

The moon was full. She turned her face towards it. A shooting star streaked across the space between the house and the neighbour's place; bright enough to show up through the town lights. When you wish upon a star . . . But the stars were too far away, and she was here, on earth, with hands smelling of fish and garbage.

She went back inside. Bernie was still sitting at the table, licking his fingers. He looked at her warily.

'Wanna cuppa?' she asked.

His face relaxed. 'Yeah. I reckon.'

She turned to the stove to get the kettle, and Bernie began to sing the national anthem.

'Australians all let us rejoice, for we are ONION FREE . . . ta ta ta da da da da something girt by sea . . . .'

The water burst from the tap into the kettle, and drowned him out.

II

During her two months of compassionate leave, Athena ran the washing machine at least once a day to keep Jessica in clean nappies. She intended to move on and get something else done while the machine worked, but after twenty minutes she would still be standing there, as though in a trance, watching while the machine swished and clicked and dribbled and vibrated.

After the first flurry of sympathy not many people visited Athena. Some people in Newera admired her. Many pitied her. Not many liked her. The exception was Rosie Thomas, who came almost every day.

For the first fortnight, Athena couldn't tell when she was speaking aloud and when words were only in her head. She was saying some awful things. Rosie sat in the living-room chair, eyes wet and feet together. Sometimes she prayed while Athena reclined lumpishly on the couch.

'You kill what you love,' Athena said to herself. 'You grasp it to you and it dies.'

To Rosie she said: 'I'm dangerous. Keep away from me. I eat people. I eat them up. I am evil.'

Rosie was scared. She sat with her hands on her lap and her feet together, the knobs of her ankle bones almost touching each other through her cotton socks.

'Why do you bother?' Athena shouted at Rosie. She was raging around the neatly seated woman, grabbing at things, shaking them, throwing them down again.

'God . . . God loves you,' said Rosie. 'He is with you.'

'Fuck, you're stupid. I hate you. I can't stand your fucking platitudes. You make me sick. You're stupid. Provincial. You stupid old bitch.'

Rosie looked at her shoes and trembled. She had seen some of the faces of grief before. She knew better than to try and staunch the flow.

Athena bent over the back of her chair and yelled 'Boo.' in Rosie's ear. Rosie jumped. 'Boo!' Rosie jumped again. 'Boo!' She jumped again. Was there no end to the woman's timidity?

There were some quiet times. Jessica was learning to walk. Clutching Rosie's bony finger, she raced around the room for hours, hauling the little bent woman after her, but the moment Jessica was left to herself, she fell over. One afternoon, Rosie slid her finger out of the child's grasp and substituted the handle of a wooden spoon. The little fingers grasped it and the baby lurched off again, giggling and gurgling, bottom heavy with nappy and one hand held over her head grasping the spoon, as though it were connected to an invisible person who would stop her from falling.

'She was born . . . .It's her birthday soon?' asked Rosie.

'Yep. Month after next.'

'Would you like . . . we could, if you like . . . we could have a party.'

Athena closed her eyes. 'I couldn't stand it.'

'I'll do it all. We could have it at Ken's place. Ken would . . . he loves children.'

'I couldn't stand it. Not people.'

'Just us then. The three of us. In the garden. You should . . . you can't just . . . .' she waved a hand around the farmhouse's gloomy interior. 'It would do you good.'

Athena looked at her daughter hanging on to the spoon.

It was a year since she had driven that sweet-smelling load of lucerne up the river and come back to find Sam and Dawn together, and almost a year since she had fought love and pain to give birth to Jessica, and the struggle between her and Sam had entered its death throes. Now here was this happy child, seemingly untouched by any of it.

She is happy, Athena thought, because I have neglected her. I have not turned myself on her. How can I be a mother? How can I love her, and let her go when the time comes. I don't know how to do these things. How is it done?

'All right.' she said. She turned away from her daughter and looked at the carpet. It was covered in crumbs and toys. The design on it blurred in front of her eyes. 'All right. Let's have a party for her.'

III

After the New Year, there was no escaping unpleasant facts. The lake had begun to empty. This was an amazing thing, and an awful one too, but it did not become generally known for some while. It was not that all the water disappeared overnight. The pipe did not swim back into view. The plain did not dry out. Only those closely monitoring the lake's growth knew there was a problem. Bruce Pierce knew. The system was fully commissioned. Enough water to fill a thousand swimming pools was surging in every day, yet the lake had stopped growing. There was only one explanation. The water was seeping into the land faster than they had predicted, and was on its way to meet the rising tide of groundwater. Soon — sooner than predicted — it would find its way back into the river.

*

On her first day back at work, Bruce offered Athena his condolences.

On the second day he told her about the lake. She looked up at him, shocked.

'But all the tests . . . how could this happen?'

'I don't know. We don't know. It's a mystery.' He pulled at his tie. 'We've never struck anything . . . something we failed to take into account.'

He was clearly unsettled by it all. 'We'll find out, of course. I must admit it's got us stumped at the moment, but it must be something in our projections that's at fault. It's not a disaster. Its puzzling.'

There were contingency plans. Bores could be sunk in a ring around the lake, and pumps used to catch the seepage and pump it back to the lake before it did any harm, or went too far.

'It's more energy. More cost. It's not ideal,' he said, fingering his tie. 'But it's not a disaster.'

Athena, he explained, had to know about the problems because as part of the promotion of the lake she was organising the making of a video. She had planned to use a helicopter to get sweeping shots of birds taking off across the water, and water skiers and windsurfers and sunbakers, intercut with scenes of Newera and the river and the ferry, and perhaps children waving from the viewing deck of the Big Orange. Now there would be machinery around the lake to dig the bores.

'The video will have to wait,' Bruce said. He paused. 'It's your department of course,' he said, 'but I think we may have to re-think the tourism side as well.' He was avoiding her eyes. 'You should go out there and have a look.' He paused. 'See what you think . . . you may be . . . see what you think.'

She left work at five, picked up Jessica, then drove east, past the farm and out towards the church. COME INSIDE! GET TO KNOW YOUR FRIEND JESUS, said the sign. She had forgotten her sunglasses, and her eyes, sensitive from lack of sleep and weeping, were hurting in the light. It was so cruelly bright.

She turned off at the dirt track down to the lake and travelled in a veil of dust over the sand dunes. Jessica was asleep in the back seat.

There it lay, the lake, fungus-green and still, its sheen broken by the tops of drowned mallee trees. She got out of the car. Strange. The lake was buzzing — monotonously, like a high-voltage power line. What was it? She kicked off her sandals and felt the sludge suck at her feet as she approached the water. The lake was not round. It had ragged edges — inlets and mini-fjords and gulfs. All these were outlined strangely in white, like the shading on a map around the colored-in continents in one of Athena's old school exercise books. She picked her way towards the water, hitching her skirt up as the mud crept up her legs. Now she was at the white outline. She touched it, then licked her fingers. Salt. Like putting your tongue on the top of a salt-shaker.

Closer, and the buzzing was louder. She squinted against the evening sun and saw the cause of the noise. She saw them coming for her — rising in great particled clouds from the water — thousands, millions, trillions of mosquitoes. There were no warm-blooded things out here, and they were ravenous. Now there were three, four, a dozen of them on her arms, and more shoving their sucking tubes through the tiny holes in the weave of her dress. She bent down and, with her finger, gouged a line where water met mud. Then she waded onto firm ground again, beyond the suck of the lake.

It was late afternoon but the heat had lost none of its intensity. If anything, as the sun sank closer to the horizon, it seemed hotter. Her skin was alive with new and erupting mosquito bites and trails of blood where she had slapped at them. She could feel her face beginning to burn, and the mud drying on her legs and cracking with the little movements of her muscles.

Salty sweat. Salty tears. The fluid flowed out of her. There would be no tourists here, no fun-in-the-sun on this lake, with its shameful, scab-like fringe of white.

She stayed there for half an hour, until Jessica woke and began to cry. In that time she saw the water drop just millimetres short of her line in the mud.

Athena began the drive home, her body oozing sweat and blood. Turning on to the highway, she had to stop and give way to a convoy of trucks — great chrome monsters with windscreen eyes, bearing down at ferocious speed, flailing her car with gravel.

To them, she thought, this place is nowhere — just an anonymous spot on a boring highway. The distances were not even measured in kilometres, but in hours. Newera was not a place. It was just three hours from Adelaide. A truck on the highway between cities was nowhere, in transit, hung between departure and destination in no-man's land. Out here the trucks seemed so angry but once they reached the city they would slow down, and obey traffic lights, pause for pedestrians and become calmer. Only when they got back to the fringe, to the wet edges of the continent, could they afford to be less savage, and stop the breakneck flight from the panic of the interior.

Sitting there, heavy-hearted, buffeted by the slip-stream, Athena suddenly saw herself as though in birds-eye view. There she was, sandwiched between arteries of road and river. It was like one of those diagrams of the human body. The landscape was like a body. She was on her little capillary of a dirt road, with the trucks surging along, not likely to be diverted into the random and broken veins of the flesh. The trucks passed, and the silence resumed.

The interior, she thought. Inside. So much more frightening than anything one might find on the surface.

She turned on to the bitumen and moments later passed by the little white church. In this nowhere land, she thought, things died too easily. Words lost their meaning. Everything lost its meaning.

The very name of the place — Newera — a slurred hope. Even God had lost his voice. He spoke, not through a burning bush but through a noticeboard. Or perhaps he didn't speak at all, but saved his voice for other wildernesses in other lands, where Easter came with spring and things died in season.

Was it any wonder that here, life was so shallow-rooted? That things died so easily? There was no meaning, no strength. The lake had failed, and the spiteful, salty tide was rising in the darkness.

Now Athena was entering the Newera irrigation area and the orchards were hung about with plumes of water, pumped, pipe to pipe, artery to capillary, from the great sluggish vessel of the river.

Athena was weeping as she pulled off the bitumen to drive down to the farm. How could she live here? She had loved Sam. She had killed him. She loved the country, and simply by being here, by eating and drinking and making her living, she killed it. The lake was dead. That wet, intimate connection, that sweet dream of control, was a stinking, dead thing. Sam was dead. Everything she had touched was dead.

That evening, when the sun was setting, Athena took Jessica in her pusher up the track from the farmhouse. Rabbits were everywhere. Sam had fought a losing battle with guns and explosives to keep them down. Now they were rampant, eating everything green. The place was going to waste. It was shameful.

She stopped to catch her breath by the corner post in the top paddock. The post was weathered and grey, cut from red gum many years ago by a farmer now dead. On one side was a mark where a branch had been lopped off the living tree. The outer skin of timber bulged over the scar. The tree had struggled to heal, but now the lips of new growth would never meet. The fencepost was a thousand shades of grey, under the setting sun, but it was all grey.

Now Athena felt grief pure and simple. There was a subterranean ache, a deep-down injured bleeding, a pain so constant it had become boring. Nothing had any form. Everything was drooping and splayed out. There was no order. There was no control. Only wilderness.

IV

In front of Athena in the shade of Ken Neil's verandah was a plate of fairy cakes and fairy bread — white, buttered, multi-coloured and now drying into hard speckled tiles in the sun. Athena was no cook but she had done her best. This was her contribution to Jessica's birthday party. The platter of figs and peaches and plums, the cream sponge cake and the home-made berry ice-cream, now smeared around Jessica's mouth, had been provided by Ken.

None of it appealed to Athena. For the first time in her life, she was beginning to lose weight. It was a strange feeling: taking up less space, feeling her clothes billow around her. She knew what was happening. She was thinking small. She wanted to disappear, to let go and have no responsibility. She had given up her battle for control.

The three adults, Athena, Ken and Rosie, sat in the shade of the verandah while the birthday girl crawled and rolled in the sun, and occasionally stood and took a step. She was naked, smeared with sunblock and ice-cream, her nipples like little coins on her pigeon chest and everything about her folded and chubby. Now she crouched between the fruit trees and picked at the ant-covered windfalls.

'Jessica! No.'

The baby looked up at her mother in surprise and, apparently without noticing, urinated on the ground. Rosie giggled. Ken remembered his own moonlit urinations, and smiled.

'No!' yelled Athena, but she didn't get up. It was so hot, and the child was happy and doing no harm.

Rosie stepped out into the sun with Jessica's hat, but the baby, now rolling under the apple tree, pushed her fist against it and knocked it off her head as soon as the old woman headed back to the verandah.

'It's a beautiful garden,' Athena said as Rosie returned.

'I get a lot of pleasure from it,' he replied.

'It must take so much work.'

'It's nice. Nice to have a garden. Very nice.' He paused. 'They say . . . I read somewhere where they say a garden is the symbol of civilisation.'

'What a lovely way of looking at it.'

'I read it. Gardens stay, you see. You can't get rid of them, when other things crumble — buildings and so on. They get overgrown, of course, but they're still there, if you look. That's what it said. This thing I was reading.'

'But here they'd die if you stopped watering.'

'Yes. I suppose so.'

Rosie closed her eyes and recited: 'The kiss of the sun for pardon, the song of the birds for mirth, you are nearer God's heart in the garden than anywhere else on earth.' She opened her eyes and smiled. 'In Sunday school,' she said. 'We learned that in Sunday school.'

Ken coughed, and said: 'So what are you going to do now, you and Jessica?'

'The farm's loaded with debt. We could sell. Wouldn't get much. Or I could take it on, pay the mortgage. But I couldn't work it as well. The mallee's already re-growing in the top paddock. There are weeds everywhere. And rabbits. I keep thinking we ought to sell.'

'You'd . . . you'd move back to the city?'

'We could. Perhaps we don't belong here. This place . . . Newera. It drove him . . . well. There are unhappy memories.'

'Ah yes,' said Rosie. 'Ah yes.'

Jessica was picking at the windfalls again, and Ken got up, his thin arms shaking as he hoisted himself out of the wicker chair, and went to take her by the hand.

'Come on,' he said to her, holding out his finger. 'Come with Uncle Ken and see the little trees.'

They toddled off together, old and young, past the vegetable beds to the back fence, where Ken had planted a neat row of glistening little gum trees. He picked a leaf and broke it, and put it under Jessica's nose. 'Lemon-scented,' he said.

They walked back towards the verandah, her hand enclosing his finger. He left her in among the sunflowers, each a metre high. Her skin was mottled with green shade and yellow reflection.

'Won't she be stung by a bee,' Rosie said as her brother sat down, 'or a snake?'

'No.' said Ken. 'I don't suppose so. She's safe.' Then he turned to Athena. 'Newera,' he said. 'It's not an easy place. It takes time to belong.'

Athena nodded. 'But he wanted Jessica to have the farm. In spite of everything.'

They were distracted by a cry from the baby. There she stood, pudgy, golden, one year-old that day. The leaves above her moved in the sun — million colored. She rolled on the ground, her skin picking up scraps of bark, loose bits of grass, even the occasional ant. Then she was up, running on wobbly legs towards Athena. She buried her face in the softness of her mother's stomach.

Athena cuddled the baby to her, feeling her warmth and unquestioning trust.

'I hope,' said Athena, stroking her daughter's cheek, 'we'll find a way to stay.'

Marion Halligan

Winner of the 1992 *Age* Book of the Year Award for her collection of short stories *The Worry Box*.

Lovers' Knots

If your house was burning down, what would you save? The money, the silver, the compact disc collection? The original Dali print? The last plate from your great-grandmother's dinner set? Standing like a spectator on the lawn, hearing the greedy eating of the flames at your possessions, smelling the noisome smoke of your belongings, suddenly you disobey. You bunch up your skirt or your shirt in a mask against the heat and run inside like a footballer ducking detaining hands, to save your precious . . . what?

The boxes of photographs . . .

From Ada the matriarch to Eva the waif, from gentle Alice to sharp-eyed Sebastian . . . a family saga reduced to the shapely form of its best stories. A novel about ways of seeing and means of living . . .

The much acclaimed writer Marion Halligan has written a brilliant evocation of life in Australia. The stories swapped between generations fill this large novel with passion and sorrow.

Marion Halligan's writing is as shining with life as the rivers that flow through these pages. The style is as polished as the amber its women wear and the story as full of pictures as the files of the photographer Mikelis who needs his camera to see the world.

Lovers' Knots is one of the year's finest novels.

'. . . crackling with life and mortality . . . Halligan's magical word pictures have that serene intensity that is now her hallmark.'

Robert Dessaix

Minerva rrp $14.95
ISBN 1 86330 159 3

Thea Astley

Vanishing Points

I feel I am a lot more warmable to than Clifford. Clifford is my husband. Well, that's a misuse of a term as well. There's nothing husbanding about Clifford, even though we are legally tied. (That word should be spelt with an 'r'.) . . .

Thea Astley, Australia's most acclaimed and awarded writer, presents two novellas which sweep the reader on sentimental journeys towards an ending rather than a beginning.

Julie Truscott, a seemingly ordinary housewife, and Macintosh Hope, a disenchanted academic, each flee from lives they cannot control. The balance of their flight is destroyed by Clifford Truscott — Julie's real estate husband and the rapacious developer of Mac's neighbouring island.

In *Vanishing Points* Thea Astley is at her best.

'. . . an ebullient wit and unflagging comic energy.'

Helen Daniel, the *Age*

Minerva rrp $13.95 pb
ISBN 1 86330 328 6